JAX

ARMY RANGERS SPECIAL OPS BOOK 6

SUSIE MCIVER

1

JAX

I looked around the area where I was to meet up with my buddies for Ryan's bachelor party. I thought I heard someone shouting, so I walked to the back where the parking lot was and looked around. I couldn't believe my eyes. Two men were fighting with a woman, and it looked like she was winning until one of the men pulled out a knife. I stepped up to save the woman, and damn it, she gave me a swift kick to my gut. The next kick landed in my neck so hard I flew back. I landed on top of the garbage can. She went to kick me a third time. If I hadn't jumped out of the way, she would have busted my balls. The other two guys ran off. "Stop!" I hissed. "Stop trying to kick me! Fuck, can't you tell I was trying to help you?"

"Help me? I thought you were one of them." She whipped out her cuffs, "You are under arrest for interfering with an arrest I was making. I was bringing both of those men in for questioning for murder. Now I'll have to hunt them down again. Except, this time, they will know who I am." Her face said everything else she wasn't saying. She was beyond annoyed.

"Where is your partner? Why would you be arresting two men by yourself?" She turned me around on the hood of her car and kicked my legs apart. She handcuffed me in an instant. My heart started beating faster than it usually did and it wasn't because I was being arrested. The instant hard-on she gave me had my whole body reacting. "Look, officer," I tried to reason.

"It's detective," she almost bit my head off.

"Sorry, I'm here for my buddy's bachelor party. I'm sorry I messed your arrest up. I'll catch the guys for you. Please uncuff me before my buddies get here. I'll never hear the end of it."

"You must not have heard me. I said you were under arrest. You may have just let two frigging killers go."

I couldn't believe it when she read me my rights. Then three vehicles pulled into the parking lot. I heard my friends laughing at something Trey said.

"Fuck, look, put me inside your car before they see me."

I watched as she turned her head and looked at all of my friends now making a b-line towards us. These were the guys I was with when we were in the service. All of us were in the Army Rangers Special Ops together. Now we own a business together. We rescued people, primarily Americans, stranded in another country. Plus, we were bodyguards for people who needed watching over. We spent most of our time together and I knew I wouldn't be living this down any time soon.

"What's going on?" Conner Murphy asked. "Is this one of your fetishes, Jax? Shouldn't she be inside for the bachelor party? Do you dance, sweetie?"

Then Ryan stepped up, "What's the problem, Detective Penn?"

"Paul Bunyan here," she pointed at me. Before she could finish talking, the guys laughed.

"You must be fearless, none of us would ever say his nickname to his face," Trey said, still chuckling.

"Just because I chose to grow a beard and a nicely trimmed one at that doesn't give anyone the right to call me names. Please tell her I'm a good guy so that she will take these cuffs off of me."

"He's under arrest for interfering with an arrest I was making."

"She was fighting two men and she wasn't winning I might add." She pulled on the cuffs hard. "She doesn't have a uniform on. What was I supposed to do, let them kill her?"

"Well, he makes a good point. If any of us saw a woman fighting two men, we would jump right in."

"These men were wanted for questioning for the homicide of a woman getting off work. She was brutally raped and murdered. Now those same two men are still out there where they can do whatever the hell they want to do. They now know I want to bring them in for questioning. They are on the run and will keep doing what they have already done, rape and murder. And whose fault do you think that is?"

"That's a sad fact, but Jax didn't know when he jumped in the fight to help you," Matt pointed out.

"If you had let me help, those two would have been arrested. Instead, you started fighting me."

"I thought you were with them, and since you are so large, I had to take you down first."

"So, do I get to go to Ryan's party? Now that you know I'm innocent."

"The thing is, I will have to report this, and when I do, my boss will want to know why I didn't bring you in."

She opened her car door, and I got my first look at her. "Mine! Fuck, did I say that out loud?"

"I think I'm the only one who heard you," Matt chuckled quietly.

Detective Penn was breathtaking, even if she was a detective. I looked at her ring finger, and I saw no wedding band. Of course, that didn't mean much these days. Maybe she didn't wear her ring on the job. Or better yet, perhaps she wasn't married. I looked over at the guys and saw Trey watching her, I knew I had to say something, or he would ask her out. He was a lady's man. Women flocked around him.

I cleared my throat. She looked at me. "Did you want to say something else?"

"Umm, yeah. Would you go out with me Saturday night?" I ignored my buddies, who sounded like they would choke on their damn tongues to keep from laughing. This woman was mine. The sooner they knew that the better, to keep Conner and Trey away from her.

"And what if you are in jail on Saturday night?" she asked.

"You mean you're still taking me in?"

"Okay, since I get it, you were trying to help a defenseless woman. I'll let you go, but I will not go out with you. I'm in a relationship."

My heart dropped until I remembered she wasn't married. She uncuffed me. "Thanks, detective. What's your first name?"

"Did you not hear the part about I'm in a relationship."

"Yes, but we can still talk to each other. How can I greet you in the marketplace if I don't know your name?"

She chuckled. She had the perfect smile. "My name is Amber Penn. What's your name?"

"Jax Black."

"Okay, Jax, you are free to go with your friends. Congratulations Ryan. How is Ashley doing?"

"She is doing good. Thank you for asking."

I watched as she climbed into her vehicle and drove away. I turned and looked at the guys. "She's mine," I warned.

"Well, I'm glad you are drawn to her. She's the woman Ashley wanted to set you up with."

"Damn, Ashley really knows me. This woman is perfect for me. I'll have to overlook she's a homicide detective. She is curvy, just like I want my woman to be."

"What's wrong with being a homicide detective? I was one for a few years, and I will tell you it's hard and dangerous work," Asher Wright said. We met Asher when we were in Nebraska to rescue Ashley. He was just the right guy to join our team at the time.

"I don't want my woman to be taking chances with her life." I knew they would laugh at that and I was right. We walked inside the restaurant laughing. All I could see was Amber. Too bad she was in a relationship. I can take time before I start pursuing her.

2

AMBER

I couldn't believe it when that Paul Bunyan (the famous lumberjack) looking guy jumped in the middle of me arresting those two men. I wanted to bring those men in and question them about the murder of a woman two nights ago. I knew they were responsible when they started fighting me. Now I would have to hunt them down again. All because Mr. Handsome wanted to protect me. Sure it was sweet of him, but he ruined my arrest. It is a good thing I managed to get the wallet from one of them, and as soon as I get home.

I guess all that pocket-picking Samuel taught us has paid off. I smiled, thinking about Samuel. My sisters and I lived our growing-up life with Samuel. He was a friend of my father's. Our father will be getting out of prison in six months. He's been in prison for twenty years for killing a man who murdered our mom. We have visited him every few months. When we moved to Maine, it became harder to go see him. We wrote to him every week to keep him up to date with what was going on in our lives.

The police wouldn't believe my father when he told

them who killed our mama. So he killed the man and asked Samuel if he would watch over us four girls. Samuel was twenty-five at the time. But he said he would watch over us until my dad got out of prison. They both thought it would only be a while. They thought he would be set free when the truth came out. But the truth stayed hidden all this time.

We were lucky to have Samuel. The State would have taken us, and I'm sure we would have been separated. He didn't work much, but he taught us how to survive. He taught us how to fight. He used to teach defense fighting when he was a Marine. He also taught us how to pickpocket, we had never done any pick pocketing until now. We knew how to live off the land if we had to. My family will get a kick out of me telling them about the handsome guy who came to my rescue. I am the second oldest daughter of Anthony and Debra Penn. Opal was the oldest, Jade was after me, and Ruby was the youngest.

Our parents were gem hunters. I can still remember running wild out in those places where our parents would dig holes, hunting for any gem they could find. We were all named after gemstones. Samuel was always with us. He was their partner until my mama got killed. We have never been back to those places. Samuel always said our parents had gemstone hunting more in their blood than he did. Samuel moved us all to the desert in Southern California.

When Opal was sixteen, she fell madly in love with a boy at school, and she got pregnant. The boy didn't want anything to do with Opal because we grew up on the wrong side of town. She became so depressed Samuel was scared she would hurt herself. So he packed us all up, and we moved to where his father lived in Maine. It was like a breath of fresh air for us, the new start that we needed.

We still live with him. He has been our grandpa from the

first day we arrived. We still all live in this huge old Victorian home in the woods of Maine. I don't know what Grandpa thinks about Samuel raising us girls but he never complained, not once. Opal's boy, Axel, is a gift to all of us. We all love him so much. He's Grandpa's best friend. They are always together. I was fourteen when we moved here. Now I'm twenty-eight. I'm not in a relationship but I always say I am, so men won't keep asking me out. My focus is my career and I don't want anyone distracting me from that.

Three of us girls look like our mother except for Ruby. We all have photos of our parents on our nightstands. Mama was an actress before she married my father. She said the producers always complained that she was too curvy. She said she looked like the old actresses who had bodies men loved. We were all tall, and just as curvy as my mother. The only one of us who didn't have auburn hair was Ruby. Her hair was pitch black like our fathers.

As soon as I walked into our house, the dogs greeted me. "Oh, I missed you too," I cuddled all of them at once. "Hello, I'm home," I called out. Axel rushed down the hallway and hugged me. "How is my favorite guy doing?"

"Grandpa came and visited my school today. He told them about when he was a policeman," he said with excitement.

"How was that?"

"It was fun. I never looked at Grandpa as a policeman before. I hope your job isn't as dangerous as his was."

"I'm going to be fine. You don't have to worry about me. Where is everyone?"

"They are in the backyard. Ruby is barbequing steaks. We are celebrating her new job."

"Oh, she got a new job? What happened to her old one?"

"I've been given a new position in my company," Ruby

said, walking into the room. "You won't believe where they are sending me?"

"What do you mean sending you?"

"I'm going to Scotland to work for a year."

I know I should have been happy for Ruby, but all I could think of was Scotland was on the other side of the earth.

"Are you going to cry? Please don't cry. It's only a year, and then I'll be back, and you can come and visit me."

"I know," I waved my hand in front of my face. "I'm happy for you. It's just so far away. You deserve this promotion. You've worked so hard. When do you leave?"

"I'm leaving next Thursday. I start work there on the following Monday."

I nodded my head. I was afraid I would cry again if I tried saying anything. This would be the first time we weren't all together. I know that seems crazy. I mean, everyone moves out and away from each other. Most of them move out at eighteen. But we never did. We went to our local college and drove back and forth every day. It had always seemed to me that when one of the family went away, they never came back, so none of us left. Stupid, right?

We walked to the backyard, and everyone was there. Our backyard was all forest. It was beautiful. Every time I walk back here, I take a deep breath and feel peace fall over me. We sat around the table eating when I told my family about the handsome man who thought he would rescue me.

"Did he ask you out?" Grandpa asked.

"Yes, he did. I told him I am in a relationship."

Samuel shook his head. "Why did you tell him that? He sounds like a good man if he tried rescuing you. Where was your partner?"

"That's what he asked. He has been transferred. His wife

didn't like him working with me. Can you believe that—she didn't even know me. I met the woman once. Anyway, I haven't gotten a new partner yet."

Samuel was frowning, "Why would you try catching those two men on your own? It might have been a good thing he interrupted you. Those men could have hurt you bad."

"I can handle myself, but you are right. I'll try not to do that again. Anyway, I was able to get one of their wallets out of their pocket. So I will at least know who one was. It won't take long before we learn the other guy's name."

"I don't like you trying to take this on without a partner."

I know he thought of my mother. She was murdered by a man they thought was their friend, but my father knew it was Trevor Matzo. His family had money, so he wasn't even brought in for questioning. So my father killed him. We lost both of our parents within a month. Samuel was still talking. "There is no telling how many women these men have killed. I'll work with you until you have a new partner."

"Samuel, I know for a fact that is not allowed."

"I don't care if it is or not. Until you have a partner, I'll be with you on every shift."

I knew better than to argue with Samuel. He worried about all of us. "I'm surprised you are letting Ruby go all the way to Scotland by herself."

"Who said she would be by herself?"

"What do you mean, Samuel?" Ruby jumped into the conversation quickly. I was glad the conversation was off of me.

"You're the baby, Ruby. I can't let you go around the world by yourself."

"I'm not going to be by myself. My assistant, Anna, will

be going with me. They have already rented us an apartment within walking distance from our office. I don't want any of you to worry about me. We can have our Zoom calls whenever you want to talk to me. Opal said she, Axel, and Grandpa will visit me when she has her vacation. She's taking a month off in three months when school gets out."

My mind drifted back and went over my conversation with Jax Black. I felt my heart flutter faster than usual when I touched him. There was somethi...

"I've been thinking about getting an apartment. We will all eventually move out on our own or with someone we love. I'm Twenty-seven. I'm old enough to live on my own. I'll miss seeing everyone every day. But it's time I move out," Jade told everyone, pulling me out of my daydream.

"What, why do you want to move out?" I asked, looking at Jade. She was a year younger than me. We were all a year apart in age.

"Amber, I know you want all of us to live together forever, but it's unrealistic. When kids grow up, they need their own life. We still love each other the same, but it's time I started another chapter in my life."

I looked at Opal. "I would never take Axel away from Grandpa," she said, but Jade's right. You're twenty-eight. Don't you want to be on your own? Do you ever think of meeting someone, falling in love, and having children?"

"I haven't met anyone I would want to live with for the rest of my life. What about you?" She ignored me.

"Maybe if you stop telling every man you meet that you are in a relationship, you'll let someone have a chance."

"How did this conversation become about me?"

"I don't know," Grandpa said, "but you can live with me forever. You can even bring your husband and kids to live here. This home is big enough for everyone. I enjoy having my family living with me."

I smiled at him, "Thank you, Grandpa. I love living with you too."

3

JAX

I stood up and cheered when Ryan married Ashley. I haven't had time today to think about Amber Penn, but as I watch Ashley wipe tears from her eyes, her face popped into my head. I wondered if she was still hunting for those killers and why the hell she was alone having to take on the two of them. I already checked her out on the internet. An uncle in Southern California raised her and her sisters. They moved to Maine when the girls were young teenagers. And now they lived with their grandfather. I decided to pay a visit and offer her my support in finding those two men. With my mind made up, I relaxed. I would get there bright and early before she left for work. I could now enjoy the rest of the evening.

I looked at the directions and made my way up into the hills. It wasn't far from my home. I lived in the mountains. I pulled into a large driveway and smiled. The house was large, three stories, an old Victorian. I could hear dogs barking inside. I knocked on a massive door, and a boy answered.

"Hello, is Amber Penn home?"

"Sure, I'll get her. Come on in." I followed him inside and two giant dogs sniffed and tried to climb me.

"You two are not the best watchdogs," a woman laughed, and when I turned around, four of them stood there. I grinned. They were all knockouts.

"What can I do for you, Mr. Black?"

"Call me Jax, please. I'm here to help you find those men. Since I jumped into your skirmish with those killers, I feel the least I can do is help you find them."

She shrugged as if I was dumb. "That would get me fired, don't you think? If I allowed someone who wasn't an officer to help me make an arrest, how do you think my boss would take that? And, how did you know where I live?"

"I have my ways. I only live half a mile down the road."

"Amber, invite your friend in for coffee."

I watched as she rolled her eyes.

She walked to the doorway. "Grandpa, he's not my friend. He's the man who messed up my arrest. The one I told you about." I looked at the other women, and they were all grinning. Her grandfather was giving her a stern look. Amber turned back to me, "Would you like a cup of coffee, Mr. Black?"

"Call me Jax. Yes, I would love a cup of coffee. I walked into the enormous eat-in kitchen and smiled. This was the most comfortable kitchen I'd ever been in. I walked over and got myself a cup, and poured some coffee. Before anyone else had a chance, I introduced myself to Grandpa and Samuel, the uncle. The sisters all introduced themselves to me, as did the young teenager.

"Why are you here?"

I looked at her like she should know why I was there. "I told you I would help you bring those men in."

"I have someone to help me already. So thank you, but no thank you."

I saw her grandpa kick the uncle. "I'll let Jax take my place until you have a partner." Then Grandpa looked at me, "Amber's partner had to get another partner because his wife didn't want him working with her. Imagine, women haven't quite changed since my days," he laughed. "It's not my granddaughter's fault that she's beautiful. All of them are."

"Grandpa, if you say one more word, I'm going to sew your lips together," Amber said, pointing her finger at him.

When she said that, I spit my coffee all over the table. I looked around, and everyone, including Amber, laughed. I jumped up and ran to the sink, where I got the dish towel and cleaned my mess up.

"You have to excuse Amber, she is the outspoken one, plus she has a very kind heart, and we love her for it. I know when she's playing with me."

Samuel chuckled. "Okay, Dad, we don't need to tell Mr. Black everything about her."

"Please call me Jax."

He looked me over from head to toe then said, "Tell me, Jax, what do you do that you can take off and help Amber find these men."

"My buddies and I have a kind of security business of sorts. We also help rescue Americans stranded in war-torn countries that we don't get along with or locked up in prisons."

Samuel looked at me with his eyebrow raised. "How do you get them out of prison?"

"We break in and take them out."

"How do you get in and out?" Grandpa asked.

"We sneak into whatever country they are in, sneak

inside the prison at night and rescue them. Sometimes we are lucky, and more than one American is there."

"Who gives you the authority to go into these countries?" Samuel asked.

"Well, we don't ask for any authority. We have people who let us know where someone is. So, unless I have to rescue someone, I'm on my own time."

Samuel looked at me. I could tell he was very interested. "Are all of you servicemen?"

"We are all ex-Army Rangers Special Ops."

"This is fascinating."

"Were you in the service?"

"I was in the Marines. I walked on a bomb, and that was it with my Marine career. I had my leg amputated above my knee."

"I'm sorry about that. I've got friends caught up in that battle and are badly injured. How are you now? You know what, you can tell me more when you join us this Friday. We have pizza every last Friday of the month down at Round Table."

"Thanks, we might do that." I smiled internally. Of course, I was going to be there. Anything to spend time with Amber.

"Aunt Ruby is going to Scotland for a year?" Axel said. "Aunt Amber cried. She doesn't want anyone in the family to move away. It makes her..."

"Axel, I will sew your lips together too. Stop telling him what my feelings are," she cut him off.

"Why, will she cry?" At that, her grandfather spat coffee everywhere. I looked at Axel, and he was smiling. He said it on purpose to see what Amber would say.

"Very funny, remember this. I owe you one." Amber

looked at me, "Are you coming, or will you sit here drinking coffee all morning?"

"Is the man you are in a relationship with not going to be upset if I'm with you," I asked, walking out of the kitchen with her. Everyone back in the kitchen burst into laughter. "Did I say something funny?"

"I can't believe you didn't notice all my family is crazy?"

"So, how are we going to go about this? What is your plan?"

"I was able to get a wallet from one of the men. I have his address. So I'm going there to see what he does when he sees me. I'm then going to take him in for questioning."

"What if he starts shooting?"

"Then I'll shoot back."

"We'll take my vehicle. Those men know yours. One thing you have to remember, a killer will notice everything about what is going down. Believe me, they know your vehicle and will be on the lookout for it. What is the address?" She didn't say anything after I opened the truck door and held it open for her. Finally, she climbed in and told me the address. I walked around to the driver's side and sat down. "Okay, this is how we will do this. I'll knock on the door. They don't know me. They know you."

"If they know me, then they will know you. You were there too."

"Yes, but I'm sure they watched you inside where the light was on and then followed you out, am I right. In other words, you set yourself up for those men to attack you."

"Listen, I'm the homicide detective. You are the man who is putting himself in my way. It would be best if you stopped telling me what to do. I'm going to get out and walk home and get my vehicle."

"Then I would be there before you. Okay, I won't boss you around. I'm sorry. I have a bad habit of taking over."

"Yes, you do. I will let you come with me today, but no more after today," she warned.

Damn, she was hot. If I let my mind drift to how hot she is, I'll never be able to get out of the car. I'm harder than hell just looking at those stormy blue eyes staring at me. I tried to shift myself where it wasn't so obvious if she happened to glance down.

"How did you get his wallet?" I started up the conversation again.

"I took it from him when we were fighting."

"Without him noticing?"

"I'm pretty good at picking pockets."

"Hmm, that's not something people are usually good at. Have you practiced the art of picking pockets?"

"No, I learned when I was young."

"Did your uncle teach you?"

"Yes, as a matter of fact, he did. Wait, how would you know to ask me that? Let me guess, you have your ways. Are there any other questions you want to grill me about?"

"No, I'm finished for now." I pulled into the parking lot of the apartment building where the man lived. I looked at Amber. She was chewing on her plump bottom lip. *Damn, that bottom lip looked delicious.* I wanted to suck on it for a long night spent having hot, sweaty sex all night long.

"Why are you staring at me?"

"I WANT you to stay here. I don't want this guy to have a chance to shoot you."

"Look, Mr. Black..."

"Jax."

"Okay, Jax, I'm the homicide detective. You are a bystander. I thought we went over this before."

There was no way I was going to get my way here. I decided to let her do her job. "Okay, you can come but stay behind me." I watched her roll her eyes and hid my smile. We got out of the car, and she followed me to apartment 13B. I knocked on the door, and there was no answer. Then I knocked again, harder this time. I heard someone yelling. I stepped to the side, taking Amber with me. I made sure she was not visible when the door opened. I grinned. "Hey, are you Steven Shelton?"

"Who wants to know?"

"I found a wallet," I squinted my eyes like I couldn't see him clearly enough to judge whether or not it was him. No, I don't think it is you."

"Where did you find it?"

"In a restaurant parking lot."

"Yeah, it's mine. I lost it the other night. Hand it over."

"Okay," I reached behind me and touched Amber. She smiled as she stepped around me. The guy thought he would run away, but she had him down faster than he could blink his eyes. She cuffed him and read him his rights. Then she called for a police car to come and pick him up.

"Your buddy already told us you were the one who killed that woman. He also told us you lost your wallet and where you live," I lied.

"That mother fucker is lying. I didn't do anything to that woman. He did all of it. All I did was watch."

"We have your DNA, so we'll determine which one is telling the truth," I said, winking at Amber.

"I might have had sex with her, but she enjoyed it. She cried for more. Gary is the one who slit her throat. My fist connected with his face, and he went down."

"Why did you do that?"

"I knew if I didn't knock him out, I would beat him to death."

"How the hell am I going to explain why you are here?"

"Just tell them I was walking by, and I saw this jerk shouting at you. No one will believe him. I recorded his confession on my phone. All we need is to wait for the other guy to show up."

"Thanks for helping me, but it ends here. I will have to go fill out some papers, and then I'll come back here to see if this Gary guy shows up. Can you send me the confession you taped?"

"Sure, give me your phone number."

"Wow, you are good," she smiled.

"I don't know what you are talking about."

"You've got to be kidding. This is your way of getting my phone number."

I threw back my head and laughed. "You are the one who wants the tape," I shrugged. She gave me her number and I sent her the confession. "I will run you to get your car when the police take him away."

"Okay, can you wait over there until they leave?"

I heard the sirens, and I walked over to sit on the bench under the tree. I watched how Amber and the police officers acted around each other. I thought they were a little jealous because Amber was a detective, and they weren't. They were there for at least forty minutes before taking the guy away. After they left, she walked over to me.

"I'm ready if you are."

4

AMBER

*H*eart, please stop acting like this right now. He is not for you. Just because your family loves him doesn't mean you do. He's bossy and arrogant. He smells delicious, and I bet he tastes as good as he looks. He smiles, and my insides melt. I have to stay away from him. He doesn't know my father is in prison for murdering the man who killed my mom.

"Amber, did you hear me? I said I'll see you when you visit me in Scotland."

"Sorry, Ruby, I was daydreaming." She smiled at me and tipped her head.

"Let me guess. He's about six-two and has dreamy gray eyes and long black lashes. He has a cute beard and black hair, and you want him immensely."

"Very funny. Just because I'm daydreaming it doesn't mean it's about Jax Black. Even though he smells so good, I could lick his entire body." My sisters laughed in unison. We were all at the airport telling Ruby goodbye. We all promised to take our vacations in Scotland where Ruby would be for the following year. "I'm going to miss you so much. Ruby, take a lot of photos for us."

"I will. I'm going to miss all of you too. Don't worry about me, I'll be fine. Think of it as if I'm going away on an adventure." She walked over to Axel. "I'm going to miss you the most. I love you so much, sweetie. I'll see you in a couple of months." Axel wrapped his arms around her. We all pretended not to see when he wiped his eyes.

Ruby wiped her tears away. I knew she was on the verge of crying if we didn't collect ourselves and make this easier on her. "You are so lucky to be going on this amazing adventure. Wow, you will have a blast. Enjoy everything you can. Make sure you visit castles, even if they are only stone walls. Can you please hug those walls for me? We love you and are only a phone call away."

"I know but I'm going to miss all of you so much," she sniffled.

"We'll miss you too but we are all so jealous of you. It's going to be amazing. Come on, you have to catch your flight now."

"Okay. Let me get going. Call me when you find out the date father is getting out of prison." Samuel walked over and handed her a present. "What is this?"

"Open it."

Ruby pulled the ribbon off, and it was a picture of all of us taken a couple of years ago. We all went to the state fair, and Axel had won an enormous giraffe. Ruby threw her arms around him and started crying.

"Stop that crying. I'll be in Scotland in three weeks. You'll be so busy you won't even miss us. Dry your eyes and get on that plane."

"I know, I'm a cry baby. I love you all. I will see you soon." We watched her walking down the ramp, then she turned and waved. I watched as she jumped over the railing and ran back to us. "Samuel, you are my father. I haven't known any other, and no matter when he gets out, you are still my dad and always will be."

Samuel kissed her and then gave her a push to hurry her down the ramp. We were all quiet walking back to our vehicle. I weaved my arm into Samuel's and leaned on his shoulder as we walked. "You will always be my dad too. I'm sorry, but I don't know that man who is my father. If he cared about us, he wouldn't have killed that man. He would have thought about his four daughters. I don't know if I want him around Axel. What if he has issues that he can't deal with? I've seen what prison does to men who've been in there for years."

"Let's give him a chance."

"How long did you know him?"

"A few years. He was a good man, don't you remember?"

"My mind is blurry. I remember my mother and you most. I do remember a man with black hair and a kind smile. That's all I remember."

"That's a start. Go through the photos again. Maybe you will remember more about Liam."

"Yes, I'll do that. I'll write to my father and ask him to share some memories with me. Maybe it will bring something back to me. He must have loved mother very much to kill someone for taking her away knowing he would be taken away from us."

"He loved her more than anything. He went crazy when they found her body. We'll talk more when Axel can't hear us."

"Okay, I have a couple of things I need to take care of when we get back." Steven wasn't telling us anything. We had his confession, but Gary was nowhere to be found.

I was in town when I saw that handsome Jax with his friends, Ryan and Ashley. Ashley smiled at me like we were old friends. "Detective Penn, how are you doing? I'm so happy to see you again. This is our friend Jax Black. Jax, this is Detective Penn."

"Yes, we've met."

"You did, when?"

"Jax tried saving me from the two men I was arresting."

Jax shook his head, frowning. "You were trying to arrest them. Both were fighting you. Besides, we got one of the men. Did you find the other one?"

"No, not yet. It won't be long now. I believe he left town and I'm going to his sister's tomorrow. I think he might be hiding there."

"I'll go with you."

"I'm sorry, but I have a partner now," I said, shrugging my shoulders and looking at him. I could smell his scent. He smelled so frigging good. I smiled at him. "I'm not sure how he is at being a detective. He's from California, and all he talks about is surfing. He said he wanted to teach me to surf. I'm hunting for a frigging murderer. I don't have time to learn how to surf. Shit, sorry, I got off track. It was a sad week for our family. My sister, Ruby, just left for Scotland. She'll be there for a year to work. We aren't used to being separated. That's silly, right?"

"I don't think it's silly," Ashley said. "You're lucky you have a sister to be close to."

"There are four of us girls and we are pretty close." I checked my watch, "Shoot, it was nice seeing all of you. I have to run," I looked at Jax. "Bye."

"Where does Gary's sister live?"

"Do you honestly think I'm going to tell you that?"

"Hey, I tried. I'll see you around, Amber."

I walked away with my wet panties in a bunch. *Damn, that man does something to me. I don't know if it's lust or what. I have never lusted after a man before. But the gorgeous Jax Black makes me have all kinds of wet dreams. I would rather have him go with me instead of my new partner.* Jeff didn't seem to have a serious bone in his body. Maybe once we were in a situation where he had to act like a real detective, he would act like he's supposed to.

5

JAX

"What the hell is she talking about? Anyone with eyes can see why he wants to teach her how to surf. He wants to put his hands all over that luscious body of hers." I heard Ashley chuckle, and I looked at her. "Why did you listen to him?" I said, pointing at Ryan.

Ryan wouldn't stop shaking his head. "We don't even know if she would have gone on a blind date, and now that we know she's in a relationship, I'm pretty sure she would have said no."

"She is mine. I don't care what she has to say about it. She knows she's mine. She just hasn't accepted it yet. Now I'll have to follow her to make sure Gary doesn't kill her."

"I can't believe you know her. I knew she was right for you. I told Ryan. We need a plan."

"No, you don't need a plan," Ryan said. "We are not getting in the middle of Jax's love life. He can do it on his own."

"Why?"

"Don't worry about why. Let's get the food for the barbeque."

"Hey, Jax, I have a great idea. Why don't you invite her to the fourth of July celebration this weekend?"

"Ashley, stay out of this."

I ignored Ryan because I knew Ashley had a perfect solution. "Yeah, I'll invite her entire family. Let's order six more steaks. I'll stop at her grandpa's house today and ask if they want to join us on the beach for dinner and fireworks." *If I have to play dirty, I will.*

"What if she says no?"

"I'll worry about that hurdle when I come to it." I smiled, thinking about what a great plan of how to get her to join all of my friends this was.

"I'm sure if she is dating someone, she'll bring him along with her."

"Ryan, let's only have good thoughts. As soon as we finish here, I'll start following her."

"Don't you think that's kind of creepy?"

"Not if her partner is a surfer and not interested in guarding her."

Ryan laughed out loud until Ashley elbowed him because people were watching. "I've never seen you like this. I'm sure you've dated almost every woman in town, so why are you like this with Amber?"

"Hell, if I know." I thought about it, and I wondered if I was overreacting. *Maybe I should back off. Sure, she's a beautiful woman, but there are beautiful women everywhere. Nope, that's not why I'm doing this. I'm doing it because she sends electricity through my body with a touch of her hand. She makes my heart pump at such a speed that I worry I'll have a heart attack. She stole my breath away from the moment I met her.*

"Did I tell you her family only lives down the street from

my place? Their running trails meet up with mine. They live in this huge Victorian home three stories high with a kitchen made for a large family."

Ryan stopped walking and looked at me. "You are starting to sound like a stalker."

"I know, and that scares the hell out of me. Okay, I'll back off. I won't invite them to the fourth of July celebration. I'll cool it and see what happens. Wow, I was turning into a weirdo there for a minute."

"Did you actually jog to their property?"

"Yeah, I did."

THREE WEEKS LATER, I still hadn't gotten Amber out of my system. I was in Washington DC, working up in the hills. I was guarding a couple of teenagers who had death threats against them because their father, who was a senator, made someone angry. We were in the backyard when I heard a noise.

I whistled, which was our plan that meant danger. They were out of the pool and went behind the outdoor kitchen without me having to say anything. First, I made sure the kids were in a safe place. Then I walked around to where I heard the noise. A damn raccoon jumped out of a tree and flew on me. I jumped, and I may have shouted. I know I scared the raccoon as much as he scared me. I still had a hold of him, so I walked over to show the teenagers what the noise was. Then I carefully let go of him in the tree again. That's when I heard it again. It was no raccoon this time. I whistled, and the kids did their thing. I pulled out my gun and stayed behind the wall. The man walked around the corner with his weapon, ready to shoot someone.

I knocked his gun out of his hand and had him down in an instant, and I hurried to zip-tie his hands and feet together. I called the police, and they picked him up. Before they hauled his ass away, he told us that he wasn't the only one hired to kill the kids. I knew what we had to do. The man who hired these people had to be found. So I made a deal with the guy I caught. He said he would tell me who the man was that hired him and in return, I'd tell the judge that he helped solve the problem. I agreed because I knew the judge wouldn't care what I had to say.

To say we were shocked to find out who was behind wanting the kids killed was putting it lightly. A sitting congressman was trying to scare the senator into voting the way he wanted him to vote. The man was arrested and started shouting that he pretended to hurt the kids. But the man he sent had already spilled the beans on video about what he was supposed to do. He was supposed to kill one kid, and he was sure that would do the job.

A week later and I still hadn't gone to see Amber. So when I saw her and a man sitting at a table in my favorite restaurant, I was surprised. I was with another woman, but I felt like a knife went through my heart seeing her laughing with another man. I know that's stupid. I mean, I wasn't in love with Amber. She told me she was in a relationship. I thought she was saying that so I wouldn't ask her out. I stopped by her table.

"Hello, Amber. How are you doing?"

"Oh, hi Jax, I'm good. How are you?" she smiled up at me.

"I'm also good." I heard a throat clear, but I didn't feel like introducing my date to her. All I wanted to do was grab the man by the throat and throw him out of my seat. I nodded my head and made my way to our table leaving them to enjoy their evening, though I wanted him gone. My dinner and my night were ruined. When my date excused herself after dinner to go to the powder room, I told her I needed to leave because of an emergency. I knew I couldn't make love with her while Amber was on my mind. Instead, I went home and jogged over to Amber's. After waiting there for almost thirty minutes, Amber was home.

"Jax, are you out here somewhere?"

"I'm right here."

"I saw that look on your face. I knew you would be waiting for me. You don't have a right to be angry at me for being in a relationship. You were with someone. We don't even know each other. Why would you get angry at me?"

I stepped up as close as I could get. "I wasn't angry with you. I was jealous. And how did you know I was going to be here?

"I saw that look on your face. Everyone did. And I know you 'have your ways.'"

"Listen, I don't want any other man touching you or taking you out on dates." Without realizing, I pulled her to me and bent my head as I whispered against her lips. She didn't back up or tell me to move. "Do you now know what I felt?" I knew she could feel my hard erection, and I didn't care. "I want you."

"You haven't been around for a month. You can't just walk into my life and tell me you are jealous," she whispered against my lips.

She didn't pull away. She wrapped her arms around me. I held her face in my hands. "You can't be with other men."

"You were with another woman. Where did you find her, at a strip joint? If I can't see other men, you can't see other women. You can't touch them. You can't be anywhere with them. I don't want them smelling you."

I chuckled. "It's a deal," I said as I devoured her mouth. It was instant ecstasy, our tongues quickly colliding, our breaths heavy. I wanted her so much my hands trailed under her top, and her breast fit perfectly in my hand. I needed to touch her everywhere. I needed to mark her as mine. She belonged to me. "Come home with me."

She surprised me, and I smiled. "I'll drive," she said against my mouth.

It took a couple of minutes to get to my house. I had her halfway undressed before we got into the house. I pushed her against the wall and finished undressing her. I looked at her. "You are beautiful."

"Let me see how beautiful you are?" I chuckled as she started pulling my clothes off. I stood naked as she checked me out thoroughly. Her hands ran over my body. She kissed all of my scars. Her hands trailed over my chest and shoulders. She kissed me as she wrapped her body as close to me as she could get. I pushed her to the wall as my hand trailed down her. I was like a teenage boy. I wanted to be inside of her so bad I had to force myself to give her pleasure before taking mine. My hand skimmed over the skin of her inner thigh. She sucked in her breath.

"Part your legs, sugar." My hand rubbed against her smooth legs, and my fingers parted her folds when she opened up for me. I gently pushed my finger inside. She was wet and ready for me. I touched her nub, and she made a noise deep in her throat. While two fingers went inside her, my thumb circled her nub. Amber called out for more as I let her have everything she asked for. My fingers were moving in and out fast.

She bit my shoulder as she orgasmed in my hand. I wasn't finished. I wanted her to come again before I entered her. While she was crying out from her orgasm, I got on my knees, and my tongue took over. I nibbled her nub as my fingers pushed inside of her. She ran her hand through my hair as I grabbed her ass so my tongue could take more. She cried out my name when she orgasmed again, then I carried her to the carpet, and my hard erection entered her. She was so tight, and I was so hard. I kissed her when I entered her. "Tell me if you hurt."

She gazed into my eyes and smiled. "Give me all you've got. I want to make love with you all night."

I kissed her deeply and pushed my erection deeper inside. Amber was making the hottest noises from deep in her throat. I almost came just from her moaning. I touched her lips with my tongue, licking her like I did the core of her.

"Faster," she demanded. I smiled as I pounded faster and harder. I was pumping hard when she orgasmed and I exploded at the same time. I cried out her name before I collapsed on her. I held myself up with my elbows so I wouldn't squash her. When my heart slowed, I rolled over still holding her close to my heart. She kissed my chest, and her arms circled me. I picked her up and carried her to my bed. This is where I wanted to keep her. We kissed, then we slept. I opened my eyes and Amber was already up. My heart raced as thoughts of our night together came rushing back to me. I was happy to see her here still. I had never stayed all night with a woman before, but I wanted Amber to stay with me forever.

"Where are you going?" I asked, watching her look around for her clothes.

"I have to get home."

"Stay with me."

She raised her head. "It's three in the morning. I need to go home. They'll worry if I don't come home."

"Why will they worry about you?"

"Because I've never spent the night with anyone before."

"Come back to bed, and then we'll get up together, I'll help you find your clothes."

She sat on the edge of the bed and kissed me. I wrapped my arms around her and pulled her under the sheet. I pulled her under me and grinned as I made my way down her body. I tasted every inch of her before I made my way back up to where she was. She looked at me and grinned. She tried flipping me on my back, so I let her. She made her way down my body. When she took my hard erection in her mouth, I closed my eyes and tried my best not to orgasm. She was killing me. She licked me, and she bit my inner thigh before I pulled her up and flipped her over. I entered her, and we made love until I could see daylight outside. When she got up and walked into the shower, I joined her, and we made love some more. I couldn't get enough of her.

"Would you like me to make you some breakfast?"

"No, I have to get home."

"I'm going with you. We'll have our coffee there with your family. Maybe Samuel will cook for us."

She chuckled. "Now, where are my clothes?"

"We took them off in the front room."

"That's right. You had me so hot and crazy that I couldn't remember where I took my clothes off," she chuckled. "Jax, I've never felt like that before. Just thinking about you makes me want you again," she bit her lip and ran her hand over her breasts. I wanted to take her right there, make love to her for the whole day but I knew we had to get going.

"If you don't get some clothes on, we will not make it to grandpa's house for another two hours." She giggled and ran to the front room. After I dressed, I followed her. She was sitting in the kitchen.

"Your kitchen is beautiful?"

"Thank you. I have a thing for kitchens. They have to be large and colorful with lots of plants." She pointed out other things she liked in the house and it made me feel good that she liked my style.

I rode with her back to her grandpa's house. The family was in the kitchen when we walked in. "Sorry I didn't call to tell you where I was."

"That's okay. I saw your car when I was on my run. We knew you were safe," Samuel said. I watched as she poured us both a cup of coffee.

"We hoped we could eat some of Samuel's delicious pancakes," Amber said.

"So when did you two get together? I thought you were going to meet John for dinner."

We were still standing in the kitchen I knew it was too easy. "When I saw Amber sitting at that table with someone else, I knew it should have been me sitting there. I'm not the kind of guy to cause a scene in public so I did what I knew best..."

"He was waiting here when I got home last night," Amber cut in. "It was my fault," Amber said, looking at me. "I was so jealous seeing Jax with that woman. I wanted it to be me. I knew he would be here; I saw it in his eyes. So when I got out of the car, I called out, and I was right. He was waiting for me. He promised he would never touch another woman, and I would never touch another man. From now on, it's Jax and me." When she finished talking, she stood in front of me. She grabbed the front of my shirt and pulled me to her, and she kissed me right there in the middle of their kitchen. It wasn't a little kiss either, she leaned into me, and I knew I had to keep her in front of me, or everyone would see my reaction. This woman was going to have her uncle take my head off right here in their kitchen.

I raised my head, but she wasn't finished. I whispered, "Sweetheart, we have company." She opened her eyes and looked like she was ready for me to make hot, sweaty skin-on-skin love with her.

"Oh, sorry," she looked like she was in a daze.

"Stay where you are, or every family member here will know what I want right now," she smiled and nodded.

"Dang, should we leave?" Axel asked.

"Axel," Opal said, but we could hear the laughter in her voice.

"I'm going to have to find me a woman," Grandpa said, chuckling.

"I'll start the pancakes." Samuel said, walking past us. "I want to say I'm glad you two are together. We like you." He bumped me on the shoulder.

I smiled. "I like all of you too."

I stayed the morning with Amber and left when Kash called us all in for a meeting. Someone needed us to get their family out of Afghanistan. It would be risky because the Taliban were watching the family closely but it wasn't the risk that I was worried about. I was used to that. I didn't want to leave when such a beautiful thing had started between Amber and me. I wanted to have her over tonight and the night after and even the one after that. I wanted to take a break from everything else and enjoy her. I was not in the mood to go out of the country now but I had to do my job.

6

AMBER

Jax had been gone a week and I missed him. I thought of him every day since our first night together and couldn't wait for him to be back. I was there daydreaming about him, getting all hot and bothered when he walked into the police station. I jumped up and walked to him. "I missed you so much," I said, standing in front of him. He bent his head and kissed me.

"I missed you too, sugar. When can you leave?"

"Let me grab my bag." I rushed back to my desk when I remembered I had to check out a homicide victim in the next town. Jeff was leaning against my desk, waiting for me. He raised his brows, waiting for me to say something. I turned back to Jax. "Oh shoot, I forgot I was leaving to check out a homicide." I felt Jeff walk up next to me. "Jax, this is Jeff, my partner."

I knew Jax was checking the blond haired detective out. He looked like a surfer, but I had to admit he was pretty sharp. "I hear you come from Southern California. You might know a few friends of mine. Do you know Emma

Stone or Skye Sun Eagle? Ash Beckham or Killian Cooper or any of the Band of Navy Seals?"

"I've heard of them, but I don't know them myself. So they are your friends? Wow, and who are you?"

"Jax Black. Nice to meet you, Jeff. I didn't catch your last name."

"It's Wilson, Jeff Wilson. It's nice to meet you too."

"Come on babe, I'll walk you to your car." Jax put his arm around me and we walked out of the station. "Call me when you get home. I have to meet with the guys at two, but I have my phone," he said, ready to walk away.

"Okay, I'll see you later today." I watched as he walked to his truck. Jeff finally got to where I was and got into the car.

"Do you know his friends?" Jeff didn't wait for me to answer. "They are well known in southern California. Skye Sun Eagle and her sister, Dakota, who is district attorney. She hates human traffickers. All the police respect all of Jax's friends." He went on and on about them until we reached the next town and went straight to the morgue. I hated walking into morgues. They were cold and downright creepy. I pushed the button, and Sheila Brooks opened the door. I walked inside, and chills went through my body.

"How can you stand being in here all the time? You are in a basement with all these bodies, and it's freezing in here." I was shivering.

"I like it here, no one to annoy me. It's dead quiet," she giggled at her own joke. "I know I'm one of the crazies. My husband makes me undress in the backyard and go straight to the shower every day when I get home. He swears he smells dead people on me."

"What do you have for us?"

"Here she is. She was a college student, and she's already been identified. Her uncle was here just a while ago. It was so sad. I swear this is what I hate about my job, facing the family members. But I'm good at what I do. Come over here, I want you to see this. Whoever killed her carved a z on her chest. Stacey was her name. She was brutally raped. There are bites over most of her body, I'll show you in a moment. Come over here and look at this." She led me over to another body she pulled out of the wall. This was a boy who looked to be around twenty. She unzipped the bag and I saw the z carved into his chest. His body was covered in bites too.

Jeff spoke up, "The killer is bisexual. He was also raped, wasn't he?"

"Yep."

"Have you called the FBI?" I asked, looking at the boy. "When was this one found?"

"Four days ago. I won't be able to release them to their family because the FBI has their own agent who will be looking them over. He will be here tomorrow."

"Do you know if he was a student?"

"Yes, they both went to our local college."

"This makes me so fucking angry. Why do people have to do this?" I was moving from one leg to the next—my attempt to stay warm, keep moving. "Okay, so we got ourselves a serial killer, and he has already killed two people in a week. We need to let the public know. The college students need to know not to go anywhere unless there are at least three together. We need to catch this bastard fast. He has a taste for killing, and it will control him."

"Where are the clothes they were wearing?" Jeff asked.

"They weren't wearing any."

"But their clothes may have been near the bodies."

"I haven't seen any. If there is any forensic evidence, it will be in. I found some hair on the male, but I don't think it belongs to him. I'm holding it for when the FBI arrives. Everything I have is in this bag. Are you going to the crime scene?"

"Yes."

"Can you check the area out and see if you think it's a crime scene or if he dropped the bodies there?"

"Why do you think he might have dropped the bodies there."

"There is no blood. You would think they tried getting away. But there is nothing, no blood other than their own, and nothing under the fingernails. It's almost like they were all wearing gloves. We have to catch this bastard before he kills anyone else."

"I will let you know what we find."

When we got to the spot where they found the girl, it was roped off with yellow tape. We took pictures, but this was not where Stacey was murdered. He dropped the body here. So whoever murdered her must have known her. *Was she at his place? Did the boy also know him?*

"We need the names of everyone these two hung around with. There would be evidence if he murdered them in his home or apartment. We won't mention that we believe they were killed someplace else. No sense in tipping the murderer off." I saw a black car drive up, and two agents got out.

"Hello, you must be Amber Penn, and you are Jeff Wilson? I'm Agent Ryan Stone, and this is Agent Leann Tally. We'll be working with you on the case. So, do you think it's a serial killer?"

"Yes, we believe it is, and I'm sure they were murdered someplace else. There is no sign of a struggle here. I'm sure Stacey would have fought for her life. When I saw her, I could tell she worked out. I'm sure she would have put up a fight, unless he drugged her."

"Humm, we'll keep this quiet. We don't want to scare everyone," Agent Stone said, nodding his head and looking at us.

"I'm afraid I have to disagree. We need to tell everyone about this. That way, the people will be on alert."

He was shaking his head. "I say we won't tell anyone we think it's a serial killer, or he will be on to us."

"I don't give a fuck if he is on to us. If it saves lives, that's all I care about." I could feel my temper boiling. My mother was murdered, and I knew it must have hurt so much when my father had to view her body. Those people did nothing because the family had money and was big shots in that county. I'm not going to let another person die if I can help it. This man acted like he didn't care if there were more killings as long as it brought him closer to the murderer. If I could do something about there not being any more killings, I would do it. My friend works at the newspapers. I'd leak it to her, and she would do the rest.

"We'll do it my way. That's why I'm here. Now, where are the bodies? My forensic team wants to examine them."

I told him where the bodies were even though I didn't want to. "As soon as he finishes, the family wants to bury their daughter."

"I'll let them know. We'll take over from here."

We walked over to my vehicle and got inside. I sat there for a moment watching the FBI.

Jeff turned in his seat and sat there staring at me. "Are we going to let them take over?"

"No, I want this person caught as soon as possible. I know there are good FBI agents. Their forensic teams are excellent, but so is Sheila Brooks. So we'll get our information from her. She will be in on all of the investigations. We won't let anyone know we are still investigating these crimes."

"That's what I was hoping you would say."

"First, let's find out who these two knew in common if anyone. Maybe they hung out with the same person. We need to be discreet. We don't want the FBI to know what we are doing."

"Where are we going to start?"

I looked at him and smiled. "How do you feel about going back to college?"

"Great! I had a blast in college."

"Okay, then back to college we'll go. I'll have to see about coloring my hair so I can fit in."

"No, don't do that," he cut in sharply. "Do you know how many people would love to have that hair color? You already look like a college student. Maybe wear clothes that will show off that body of yours."

I gave him a dirty look. "I am not showing my body off. Not all college students are into that, so I don't have to be." I didn't want him getting any ideas. "I'm going to write up today's work. Then I'm going home. I'll see you in the morning." I parked the car and went into the building.

"Penn, Wilson, I need to talk to you."

We both looked at each other, then walked into the office and sat down.

"Shut the door." Jeff did and sat back down. "Tell me what the FBI said?"

"They said we are off the case, and they don't want to tell the community about the two people that were killed the same way."

"Them idiots. They come into our county and think they know what is best for us. What are you going to do about it?

Wait, don't tell me. I don't want to get involved. Catch this bastard and hang him by his balls. That's all I wanted, wait, if you need to write anything about this case that is not a case, do not bring it into the office."

"Yes, sir." When we walked outside, I stopped and looked at Jeff, "How about we drive to school together. You can pick me up in that hot car of yours. Don't forget to put the surfboard on top of your vehicle. Bring your recorder, that way, we won't have to write important things down."

"Are you going to be my girlfriend?"

"No, I'm your neighbor, who you give lifts to school."

"Okay, I'll see you around eight."

"I'll meet you here at the precinct. We'll have to think about how we get in without actually registering."

"If you walk with a crowd, you can walk right into class. I've done it before. I was trying to find a rapist. I knew he had to be in school, so I went back to high school and it wasn't too difficult to just be there. Quite dangerous when you think about it but works in our favor."

"Oh, wear your hair straight. Most college girls don't bother curling their hair. They wear it straight."

"That would be great, but mine is naturally curly," I shrugged. "See you tomorrow." As soon as I got into the car, I called Jax. It went to voice mail. "Hey, I'm on my way home. I'll see you later."

7

JAX

All I wanted to do was hold Amber in my arms. Instead, my buddies and me sat around my kitchen table talking about a college student who was murdered. The FBI was in on it, but her uncle wanted us to find the killer and make his death painful.

"Eddie, we don't kill people, you know that."

"Then bring him to me, I'll kill him myself. Catch him before he kills anyone else. The fucking FBI isn't telling us anything. I guess they don't have anything to say to us. My sister is a damn mess because of this. Stacey was their only daughter. Do you think she will ever get over this? She's just as dead as my niece is. I want him dead!" He looked at us. "I know you will do everything you can to get this guy, but don't let the FBI know what you are doing."

I looked at Eddie. He went to school with hunter and me. We knew every member of his family. "We don't hunt killers down. We'll do this for Stacey because we want to. The FBI won't know we are anywhere near them. As far as killing the bastard, we are not hired guns, but if any of us feel threatened, we'll do what we have to do to save our lives."

"Thank you. I have to get back. My parents will already be there." There was so much pain in his voice, I'd never seen him like this before.

"Eddie, tell Millie and Frank how sorry we are that this happened." He nodded his head and left.

When he was gone, we planned. That's what we were good at. You have to prepare before walking into a fire with your eyes shut. "He must be a student. Stacey told her mother she was meeting a friend for coffee. Then she would be home. She never came home, and she never answered her phone. I wish we could get on campus and ask a few questions. How about we meet up at seven—" Amber flashed in my head— "No, make that eight. We'll walk around the campus and listen. We will take a book and act like we are reading."

"Sounds good to me," Hunter said, getting up. "I say we call it a night."

As soon as they left, I jumped into the shower. As I was dressing, I noticed I had a message. It was from Amber. I finished up and jumped in my truck and went to bring her to my house. I wanted some alone time with her. I pulled into their long driveway and saw Axel playing basketball alone. I walked up to him, and he tossed me the ball. The game was on. I never laughed so hard; Axel was a shifty player. If you weren't careful, his elbow would find your side. He elbowed me so many times I knew I would have bruises. When I finally called a halt to the game, I noticed Amber, Samuel, and Opal sitting on the porch watching the game.

"Now you see why we don't rush out here to play. We

have to give our ribs time to heal. He's as tall as me, and his elbows are sharp," Opal said, laughing.

I joined in on the laughter, knowing she was on the money. "That was the best time I've had in a long time. Thank you, Axel. We'll have to do this again."

"Yeah, I won't elbow you next time. Samuel taught me how to play," I looked over at Amber and Opal, laughing as I remembered that Samuel taught her how to pickpocket. I wondered how he learned everything he knew. I bent and kissed Amber right there in front of everyone. I didn't want to wait until we were alone.

"Come and eat dinner with us, Jax," Grandpa called from the open door.

"Hey, you don't have to ask me twice. I haven't eaten since this morning. It smells delicious. What is it?"

"This is my famous barbeque ribs. The meat is so tender it falls off the bone. Sit yourself down and dig in after we say our prayers."

"Axel, can you say grace?"

"Yep," he closed his eyes, and then he prayed. "Lord, thank you for helping me win at basketball today, and thank you for giving us Jax for a friend. Thank you for the food lord, and thank you for Grandpa. Amen."

"Dig in, Jax," Grandpa said. I was stunned that Axel gave thanks that I was his friend. I wondered if he knew Emily's sisters and brothers.

"Do you go to school with any of the Jones kids? There is Kelsey, Brian, and Jason. He is off at college right now, and then there is Mikey and Tommy."

"Yes, I know the boys. I knew them when their parents died. That was sad for them. How do you know them?"

"They are all my friends. Kash and Emily are married, they are her siblings," I said, looking around the table.

"That's right, Kash is an Army Ranger. I had forgotten about that. So you know Hunter and Charlie. They are part of the team you work with?" Amber asked.

"Yes. Do you know them?"

Amber shrugged her shoulders. "I've met them. I don't really know them. Charlie had some problems a while back, and I know Emily because of school. I've met Kash, and I met Hunter when he was after whoever was hunting for Charlie."

I put my hand over my mouth in realization. "I just grasped that you and your sisters have the names of gems. Was that done on purpose?"

"Yes, my parents liked to dig for gems. So each daughter was named after a gem."

"Did they have any luck gem digging?"

"I don't know. Samuel, did they have any luck digging for gems?"

"They would find some here and there. They weren't getting rich off it. But they loved digging and would get so excited when they found the smallest gem. They didn't need to dig for money. They had a large farm and could support themselves from that." Samuel smiled and it was evident that he remembered them fondly, "I loved watching Grace's face when she would find something. Liam sometimes would find a small gem, and then he would put it where Grace was digging, so he could see how excited she would get."

"They sound like they were very much in love."

"Liam loved Grace more than anything in the world."

"I'm sorry, this must bring up sad memories for all of you," I said, looking at the sisters.

I watched Amber. I have never heard her mention her parents. She looked at me.

"I don't remember a lot. I remember my mom more than my dad. She was always singing whether she was in the house or the field digging. We look like our mom. Ruby has hair like our dad. Other than that, she looks like Mom also."

"She must have been a beautiful woman because all her daughters are beautiful."

"Thank you," the sisters said at the same time.

"I never met them," Axel said. "But when Liam gets out of prison, I'll meet him then."

I choked on my food. I looked at Amber. "Your father is in prison? I thought he was dead. How long has he been in there?"

"Yes, he killed the man who killed my mother. He's been in there since I was five. He's supposed to get out in a few months. I don't know how I feel about that. I think of Samuel as my dad. I don't know Liam."

"So, Grace was your sister? I asked, looking at Samuel."

"No, I was their friend."

This was getting more and more bizarre. Why did I think both of Amber's parents were dead?

Samuel was still talking. "Liam told me what he planned to do. I must say I didn't believe him. I told him he would go to prison. The man who killed Grace, his family, ran half the state. They had loads of money, and they weren't doing anything about Grace's murder. The police weren't even investigating it. They were saying it was a drifter going through town. Liam took the law into his own hands. He asked me to watch the girls until he got out. He thought they would let him out in a few years, but it was never investigated because the man's father had the district attorney in his pocket. Even the lawyer Liam had was bought off."

I was shocked on hearing all of this. I had no idea. "How old were you when you took over the girls' care?"

"I was twenty-five. I would have done it at any age. I love the girls. I wouldn't let the state have them. We moved away and eventually came back here to my home."

"Why didn't you bring them here first?" I caught myself quickly. "I'm sorry, I have no right to ask questions. Forget I asked anything. This food is delicious," I said, trying to keep the mood lighter.

"It's okay, Jax. It wasn't a secret. We just never talked about it before. But now that he's getting out, I guess we'll have to talk about it. We write to each other every month. We visited him a few times. But our father didn't want us to see where he was. Samuel told us for years that he was away working until we were old enough to know that wasn't true."

"Let's enjoy dinner," Grandpa said, patting his tummy. You will all love my desert. I want you to know you are my granddaughters, and Axel is my grandson. I love all of you so much, and when Liam gets out, that will not change. This is your house. I want you always to consider this your home."

Opal jumped up and hugged him. "Grandpa, you will always be my grandpa as Samuel is our father. I don't want that man to be hurt, but he didn't think about his four daughters when he decided to kill someone knowing he would have to spend time in prison."

"That is my feelings also," Jade said. "Samuel is my father. I don't want to think about Liam disrupting our lives."

I watched Amber as they talked about her dad. I can't even imagine what she was feeling. My family was all pretty close. We thought my brother was killed overseas, which almost destroyed my parents and me. Thankfully, he was alive. The band of navy seals saved him from a prison in a war-torn country.

"Maybe we should talk about everything when Liam gets out. He won't have money or a place to live. Perhaps he won't come here, but we need to talk about what to do if he does come here," Opal said as she looked at her sisters. "I don't know what I want."

It was Amber who responded first, "We should have been planning for this long ago. Why don't we rent Liam an apartment? When he gets out, he'll have a place to live if he comes here."

"That's a great idea. I'll look around and get started on it," Jade said, looking at everyone.

LATER THAT NIGHT, we were lying in bed, and I couldn't stop thinking about one thing. Eventually, I asked her, "Why did Samuel wait so long to bring you here to raise you? Where did you live when he took you from the farm that was your home?"

"We rented that land. We had to leave because the State wanted to take us away. We lived in a small cabin in the desert for a long time. That's where Samuel taught us everything about fighting and taking care of ourselves. He showed us how to live off the land if we ever needed to. Thankfully, we never had to use those skills."

"But he could have brought you here."

"No, he couldn't bring us here at that time."

"Why not?"

"Because Samuel was kidnapped when he was nine years old, his family was on vacation at the Grand Canyon. Samuel went into the bathroom, and a man grabbed him and threw him in the trunk of his car. He kept Samuel with him for five years. The man went to work one day, and

Samuel packed his few clothes and walked away. He made it to Las Vegas, where he lived on the streets. He made a friend who talked him into going back to school. Samuel couldn't remember where he had lived before. He knew the man had taken him from his home, but when he told a teacher at school the man who stole him wasn't his dad, she simply said, 'We can't all live with our father.' She didn't look into it or anything.

"After that, he knew he would have to do everything on his own. He was thirteen at that time. He lived on the streets for two years until he moved in with his buddy and my father, Liam Penn. They joined the Marines together. Samuel was told his parents died, and he believed it. After all, he was only a child."

She was looking at me and I was nodding but I wanted her to know I was hanging on to her every word, "Okay, I am listening..."

"Then, after everything happened with my parents, we lived in the cabin. It was three rooms. When Opal became pregnant, he knew the state would take us from him. He decided to check and see if his parents were dead, as he was told. He found his father was still alive. Grandpa was very surprised when we all showed up here. He cried for weeks. He didn't hesitate to take us into his home, and he told us daily how happy we made him."

"Wow, I'm speechless..." I really was. "What a sad life Samuel lived. I'm glad he had all of you. His poor parents. When did his mom die?"

"She died two weeks before we showed up."

"Oh my God, that's so sad. She didn't get to see her child."

"Nope, Grandpa said she was never the same after Samuel was taken. He said she was on the internet all the time hunting for her son because she always believed that he was out there somewhere."

"What a sad life for all of them. I'm so thankful that he could take care of you girls. The State would have taken you away and split you all up. I'm glad you are with me." I now understood the careers the sisters had. Opal was the district attorney. Jade is a public defender. Amber was a homicide detective, and Ruby... "What does Ruby do?" I asked.

She looked puzzled but then she answered, "Ruby is a private investigator. She works for the government most of the time investigating corrupt politicians. She's training people right now in hand-to-hand combat. Ruby is one of the best fighters you will ever meet. She can fight better than most men. We all learned to fight. But Ruby learned how to fight dirty."

I pulled Amber into my arms and held her, thinking about that scared little girl who lost both of her parents at the same time. Thank God for Samuel. I shook my head, thinking about him. Who was that man who took him, and who was that fucking teacher that a child told the man he was with wasn't his dad, and she didn't do a fucking thing? I'll tell you who she was. She was someone who didn't give a damn enough to ask him what he meant.

8

JAX

The minute I got to Ryan's, I told him the story about Samuel and the girls. He would keep it between the two of us. I knew he wouldn't tell anyone. He was one of the best investigators I knew. He had everything he needed on his computer. He could hack any computer on this planet. The first thing he was going to do was find everything out about Liam and Grace Penn. Then he would see who signed Samuel into school when he was in Southern California. I wanted to know who that teacher was that didn't help a scared little boy.

"I'll do Samuel first. I'd love to get my hands on that man who kidnapped him, and that teacher will regret not paying attention to a small boy who asked for help."

"I knew you would understand how I felt. Thanks, Ryan. If you need me for anything, let me know."

"I might have to ask Amber a few questions."

"Let me know what they are, and I'll ask her. Her mother's name was Grace. I don't know what happened to her side of the family. Maybe she didn't have any family members. I'll ask Amber and see what she says. This is becoming stranger every day. If Grace has family, why weren't they the ones to raise the girls? I mean, Samuel did a terrific job of raising them. I doubt anyone could have done a better job. They love him as if he was their father. Opal has a son. But if anyone was hunting for them, all they would have to do is look up their last name."

"Do you think they might have changed their last name?"

"I hope not. That would be getting into something illegal, and I don't want that to happen. If anything like that comes up, we'll shut this investigation down. The girls are too happy to destroy it right now."

"How did Samuel and Liam meet?"

"When Samuel lived on the street, Liam befriended him. He let him move in with him, and they joined the Marines together."

"Okay, that's useful information. I could start by checking out their Marine records. Now you've got me curious."

He walked to his office and turned his computer on. He brought up the Marine roster and looked for Liam Penn and Samuel Green. Samuel came up right away, but he couldn't find Liam Penn anywhere.

"Do you think he changed his name? He could have done that."

"Why would he? Unless he was in witness protection and they changed his name. But that would be blown to hell after he killed that guy."

"I don't know, Jax, but I'll see what I can find. It looks like we might be opening up a hornet's nest. Are you sure you want to do this?"

"Now I'm surer than ever. Samuel raised the girls, this man who is their father hasn't seen them in twenty years.

He's been in prison, and I want to know everything about him. Now I'm wondering what all Samuel knows. If they lived together when they were younger and joined the service together, he would know his real name if he had it changed."

"Very intriguing. Can I ask Brinley to look something up if I need to?"

"As long as she keeps it to herself, I don't want other people involved if he is under the Witness Protection Program. Call me when you find something. Thanks, Ryan."

"Don't thank me yet. I haven't found anything."

"But I know you will."

"Yes, I will. I'll see you around. Oh, before I forget, you should ask Amber to the barbeque this weekend. We can all get to know her."

"Yeah, I will. Maybe I'll ask the whole family over. Well, except for the youngest sister; she is in Scotland working. She'll be there for a year." It dawned on me just then. "Ryan, here's a clue. They are four sisters and they all look alike, except for Ruby who has black hair. Amber told me that their father has black hair like Ruby, so if you see a picture of him, he will have black hair..." I paused as I shrugged at that. Time had passed, the girls were women now. "Never mind, it might be gray by now. Listen, I'll call you later unless you contact me first. Another thing, they have never been apart. They have all lived together always. With Ruby going to Scotland, it's the first time they've been apart."

"That's different. How come? I thought they were grownups. What about when they went to college?"

"They all went to the local college and drove to school back and forth every day. Ruby is a hand-to-hand combat instructor. She is a private investigator for the federal government mainly on corrupt politicians. She does do some investigating for private companies once in a while. She's twenty-five."

"So all of them are in the business of rightness. I'm not sure that's the word I should use, but it all boils down to that."

"Yes, they are all in that business. I thought the same thing when I heard about their occupations. Anyway, I'll see you around," I finished, walking out the door. I hoped like hell I didn't regret what I was doing. I hoped I didn't have to tell Amber what I was doing. I was sure she wouldn't like the idea that I was checking her family out. I just wanted to get to the bottom of something that was bothering me. I enjoy being with Amber. I'm not saying I want to marry her. I doubt that I will ever get married. I have never had that feeling that I want to spend the rest of my life with one person. I broke my train of thought and called Amber.

"Hello."

"Hi sugar, what are you doing?"

"I'm on my way to investigate a shooting in the mountains. It's in an area where the mountain people like to take care of their own business. But this time, a new neighbor moved in, and she didn't like the idea of the mountain people taking care of a shooting. She said a woman was murdered and no one would call the police."

"That's something you have to be careful with. Those people have lived their way for a long time. They have always taken care of things their way."

"Well, not this time. Now I have to find out who murdered a woman and arrest whoever did it."

"Where is Jeff?"

"He has the flu."

"Come by, and I'll go with you."

"I'm already almost there. I'll call you when I get home."

"Amber, don't get anyone in those mountains mad at you."

"I'll try not to."

"Bye," I wanted to say more. I almost said, 'I love you.' That would have been way out there. Amber probably would have run as fast as she could. *I'll invite them to the barbeque on Saturday.* With that thought in mind, I went home and did laundry and cleaned the house. It was almost nine when Amber called.

"How did it go?"

"The family had already buried the aunt in the family plot on their property, can you believe that? I asked how she died, and they said it was already taken care of. And damn it, I'm going to piss all of those mountain people off because I will have her body dug up and see exactly what she died from. So, tomorrow ten of us will be there. Her nephew told me a doctor examined her and pronounced her dead from a gunshot wound. But he wouldn't tell me anything else. She was thirty-seven."

"Damn, maybe you should let them take care of it."

"I can't do that. I'll talk to you tomorrow."

"Amber, I wanted to see if all of you want to come to a barbeque on the beach Saturday."

"That sounds like fun. I'll ask and see what the others say." We hung up, and I had already decided to be at her house at six the following day.

I RANG the bell and waited for someone in the house to open the door. It was Amber who came. "Hi, sweetheart," I greeted her.

"Jax, what are you doing here?"

"I'm going with you today."

"I'm afraid that won't be possible. Jeff is going with me today and a few others. Come in and have some coffee and breakfast. Grandpa is cooking."

"Yummy. What are we having?" I asked as I pulled her into my arms for a long hot kiss. My hands slipped up under her sweater when I heard someone talking. I stepped back and then gave her another quick kiss.

"Bacon, eggs, and biscuits," She took my hand and we walked to the kitchen. The rest of the family greeted me, and grandpa poured me a cup of coffee as I sat down at the table. I felt a little guilty knowing I was investigating the family. But I knew I had to see what wasn't connecting. Something in this story didn't fit into place. I hoped I was wrong, and everything was as Amber and her sisters thought—that their father killed someone who killed their mother. I hoped nothing sinister was involved. I just didn't like the look of things. It wasn't making sense.

"What are you doing up so early, Jax?" Jade asked.

"I was going to tag along with Amber, but she says her partner will be with her today. Did Amber get a chance to tell you about the barbeque Saturday?"

"Yeah, it sounds like fun. You can count us in. What should we bring?" Opal asked.

"Just yourselves."

"I'll make something special," Grandpa said, pulling out a small recipe box. I looked at Amber, and she was smiling. She loved her family. There was no way I was going to come between them, but I needed to get to the bottom of things.

9

AMBER

I couldn't believe these people thought they could take the law into their own hands because they lived far up in the mountain. God, there was no talking to them. The doctor and the mortician gave us all the papers on her death but she wasn't examined by a homicide detective. They didn't even take photos. I know the people who live in these Appalachian Mountains think they don't have to talk to me, but the law is the law and they were by no means exempt from it. For three days, I tried talking to them. Finally, I decided to speak one-on-one with the man who seemed to have the say up here. I left early Friday. Jeff went to the hospital last night with a ruptured appendix. So I was on my own today, and I planned to talk to the man—Donald Abbot.

I drove way up into the Appalachians. People must have heard I was coming because men walked out of the woods as I drove past them. I was a little leery now. I didn't realize it was so far. *Maybe I should have gone by and asked Jax to come with me. Stop it, Amber. You'll talk yourself into being scared. I think I'm lost. I'll stop and ask the next person I see where Donald lives.*

I saw a woman standing on the side of the road. I slowed down and rolled the window down. "Hello, excuse me; can you tell me where Donald Abbot lives?"

"Why are you even coming here? He ain't gonna talk to you. Go home. We take care of our own here."

"Can you please just tell me where he lives."

She looked around as if she was checking to see if anyone was watching then she replied, "I'll take you there." She opened the door and jumped in.

"Hmm, okay. What's your name?"

"Why are you a detective? You are beautiful. You could be a movie star. Your figure is like Marilyn Monroe's. Quit this job. I been thinking about you and I don't want you getting hurt."

"Why would I get hurt?"

"I've heard things."

"Like what?"

"Don't worry about what I heard. Pullover here. Donald lives down that road there. Don't do anything stupid." She got out, turned, and walked back towards where I picked her up.

The trees were so thick here it was like driving in a dark tunnel. I was starting to wonder if my phone would even work here. Three large dogs ran to my car before I saw the house, then I saw the man standing on the front porch of a beautiful home. There was seating around the porch, it looked like it wrapped around the entire home. I saw a swing seating that looked comfortable. He called the dogs and put them inside the house.

He waited until I opened the door, then he stepped down. "What can I do for you, Detective Penn?"

"Are you Donald Abbot?"

"I am."

"I understand you are the law up here."

"I'm only a man everyone talks to. Come and sit down. I'll get us some iced tea." He disappeared for a minute or so then returned to the room where I was. I was still standing, waiting for him. I wasn't planning to have his iced tea either. I just needed him to answer my questions so I could get on with solving my case. He took a sip from his glass before saying, "They come and tell me about what goes on up here. I'm not any law. My father took care of things here. He died last year. I don't want the job they are trying to push on me. I'm a writer, so I'm not that social. The mountain folk thinks I took over from where my father left off. I haven't. I'll tell you what I know about the woman who was shot. I did take lots of photos. Have a seat, and I'll get them for you."

This time, I took a seat and admired the quilts folded up on the table. I raised my head when he came back. "These are beautiful."

"Thank you, my great-grandma and my grandma made them."

"So what happened to this woman who was shot?"

"Her daughter killed her. Wanda beat her daughter severely and she was disabled with broken bones that were never set. So, I'm sure you can imagine what her body looked like. Girl, that is the only name she had. She was fine when her father was there, but he left them. He ran away with another woman, and Wanda took it out on her daughter. Everyone thought Girl went with her father until she killed her mother."

"That's horrible. Where is the daughter now?"

"I took her to a hospital where she could get some help."

"Wanda deserved what she got, I'm not saying she

deserved to die, but I am the one who helped the daughter. She was starved and beaten so severely that she couldn't even walk. I knew she couldn't be questioned, so I took it upon myself to get her some help."

"I agree with you. I can't imagine what she went through. The poor thing, how old is she?"

"Sixteen, she's been chained up most of the time. She told me this was her only chance to escape."

"Wow, where did they live? I'll take your photos and photos of their home, and the case will be closed."

"Their home was burned down by the women who live up here. They feel guilty because they never checked on Girl. They are even mad at themselves because they never did anything about her name. It doesn't surprise me that they wouldn't talk to you."

"I wish I had this information from the beginning. I would have closed this case sooner. Thank you for talking with me."

"Detective, be careful who you talk to up here. Some of these people have never been out of the Appalachians. I don't know what they would do if they believe you're going to cause trouble."

"You can let all of them know the case is closed."

"Let me get those photos for you."

I left Donalds's home and headed out back down the mountain. It was starting to get dark. For some reason, it got darker faster in the mountains. I hadn't eaten anything since this morning, but I decided to keep on driving. I called Opal to fill her in on what happened. I told her everything. She told me to come straight home instead of stopping somewhere to eat. I agreed and kept driving. Until I was hit from behind. My car swerved and hit the side embankment. I looked around, and car lights shined in my eyes. I made sure my gun was ready. I tried moving my car, but the truck kept pushing me further off the road. I knew there was a drop-off, and if they kept it up, I would fall down the side of the mountain.

"Fuck, are they trying to kill me?" I shouted to the inside of my car. "Stop right now!" I rolled my window down and shot at their vehicle as I went over the side of the mountain. I hit something, and my airbag exploded in my face. I know I stopped breathing for more than a minute. I just had my life scared out of my body. Now I wondered what stopped my car from going down the rest of the way. I couldn't see anything. There were no glares from people's porches or street lamps. Just me and Mother Nature, so that means no lights.

I took my flashlight from the pocket in my car door and, moving carefully, I shined the light out from my window. My car sat on a massive boulder, which was the only thing keeping me from falling the rest of the way down the mountain. *I have to get out of here before the car falls off the rock. How am I going to do this?* The window was opened, and I crawled slowly out of the window. When my top half was out, things happened. As soon as my hands touched the boulder, the car rocked. I screamed before I lunged myself out the window. My car flipped over and fell the rest of the way down the cliff face. I sat on the rock, afraid to breathe. I knew I'd be here until I was found. It was a miracle that I landed on this rock.

10

JAX

I knew Amber said she would call me when she got home, but it was close to midnight and she still hadn't called, so I went to see if she was home. Opal was getting into her car.

"I was just coming to see you," she said, getting back out.

"Where is she?"

"I don't know. She called me three hours ago, and she was on her way home. She won't answer her phone. I'm worried something has happened to her."

"What did she say when she called you?"

"That she talked to a man named Donald because she heard people went to him when there was a problem. He lives far up in the mountains. And she told me about the girl and her mother; the woman who the girl shot and killed."

"We need to visit this Donald person and find out where Amber is or I'm going to knock some heads together. Do you want to come with me?"

"Yes, let me tell the others." I walked her back into the house. "I'm going with Jax to find Amber."

"Let me grab my sweater," Jade said. "I'm coming with you."

Grandpa and Axel stayed behind, the rest of us left to find Amber. We would find her or this someone named Donald would be fighting for his life.

"Damn, it's dark up here," Samuel said, breaking the silence in the car. His head poked out the window.

"Where is Jeff?" I asked out loud for anyone to answer.

"His appendix burst, and he's in the hospital. Amber was alone today."

I couldn't believe she came up here on her own. "We'll have to have someone show us where Donald lives." We drove for another hour when we saw a woman walking on the side of the road. "Why would she be walking out here alone. Let's ask her if she knows where Donald lives," I said as I slowed down and rolled my window down.

"Excuse me, can you tell me where Doanld lives?"

She looked at us, and then she pointed her finger, "You have to drive until you see the tree that looks like a wishbone. Then you turn on the dirt road and go another mile.- Donald's house is in the meadow. You can't miss it if you turn down that road."

"Thanks." I drove with my high beams on so that we could see the trees. I hoped to hell she wasn't pulling my leg.

"Wait," Jade called from the back seat, "I think we just passed it." I backed up so I could shine my lights on the tree. It felt like we had been driving for hours hunting for that damn tree. It was late, and the longer I was away from Amber, the angrier I became.

That looked like a wishbone tree to me. We turned down the dirt road. We had gone about half a mile when three large dogs started barking and tried to bite the tires on my truck. I rolled my window down. "Get the fuck away from my tires, or you will get run over."

"There is his house," Opal said, opening the car door.

"Opal, wait, we don't know who's here," Samuel said, stepping in front of her.

"Fine."

I looked at Opal and knew her teeth were grinding together. She didn't like Samuel treating her like she couldn't take care of herself. But she loved him, so she would do as he asked and walk behind him. We all saw the man on the porch.

"How can I help you?" he said as he stood with a rifle in his hands.

"We're looking for Detective Amber Penn. She came to see you and hasn't been seen since."

"Fuck, I told her to be careful. Come in, and I'll call a few people." He lowered his rifle. I was surprised this went so easy. We followed him inside, he picked up his phone and dialed some numbers. He turned around, that's when I saw his face.

"Donald, I didn't know you lived in these mountains." I hugged my old friend.

"Jax, good to see you old friend. I didn't recognize you in the dark. So you know Detective Penn," he said when we broke from each other's embrace.

"Yes, how long have you lived here?"

"I moved back a couple of months ago when my dad died."

"I'm sorry about your father."

"We are all going one of these days. He lived a long life. I hope your detective friend is okay.

"She better be. If someone on this mountain has laid one finger on her, I will kill them.

"Yeah, it's been so long since I've been here, I forgot how they are. My dad always said if he didn't act as the law up here, they would kill each other. I'm going to tell you right now, no matter what these people think, I'm not going to act as my father did. I love this home. My great grandfather built this house. I had hoped I could live here quietly. I won't get caught up in all of the drama in these mountains. I'm a writer and all I want to do is write."

We talked some more but his phone never rang. As the time passed, he too seemed to get on edge. He went back over to the phone and I watched as he called at least six people before someone talked to him. I saw his face. He was angry, and then he exploded. "Meet me at the end of my road," he hung up.

"Tell us."

"The person I talked to said they saw some trucks pushing a vehicle off the side of the cliff..." I heard Jade and Opal cry out at the same time. I counted to ten before I said anything.

"She better not have a mark on her, or I will fucking kill everyone on this fucking mountain who has a truck."

I walked out the door, followed by Samuel, Jade and Opal. Donald ran and jumped into his vehicle. We followed behind him. When we got to the end of his driveway, I saw a woman jump in his car. We drove about six miles when he pulled off the side of the road. I could see broken tail lights where someone hit her car. The sun was already coming up, so we could see much better now. There was an old bumper that must have belonged to the other vehicle. As soon as I found my woman, I would be taking that back with me. Those bastards would hang, even if I had to do it myself.

I shined my light down the mountain. We didn't need it; we could see clearly now. I saw Amber's vehicle at the foot of the mountain. It was smashed to pieces. I roared so loud the trees shook. Jade and Opal cried out and followed me down the cliff. I shouted at them to get back up, but they ignored me. Doanald was right behind them. "Fuck, are we all going to roll down this mountain together?"

"Amber, can you hear me, sweetheart?" I called out in the loudest voice I could muster. I refused to believe she was dead. We all called her name. I looked at the sisters. "Stay here. It is too steep for you to go down any further. I need you to help Samuel get the rope out of my truck." I ran my fingers through my hair, my hands were shaking. I couldn't lose her. I had just found her.

"Amber, can you hear me? Answer me," I called again. "Damn it," I said under my breath.

"Stop shouting, she can't hear you," Opal cried out. She fell forward and Donald grabbed her from behind.

I walked another twenty feet down and knew it would be almost impossible to go further. I would have to call in a helicopter. I put my hands around my mouth and shouted, "Amber!" I held my hand up to silence everyone because I heard something.

"Jax, I'm behind the big rock. Hang on, I'll come..." I didn't let her finish. I slid down the cliffside and saw her trying to make her way up.

"Sweetheart, thank God you are alright," I said when I reached her finally. I pulled her into my arms and held her tight. I never wanted to let her go. "God, I was so scared."

"Me too," she said. "I stayed behind the rock so those trucks wouldn't see me. There were two of them. Those fuckers pushed me off the road."

"Can you climb up beside me? I'll carry you if you can't."

"Yes, I'm not hurt. I might have some bruised ribs, but that's from the airbag. She wiped a tear from her cheek.

"That was a close one." I could hear Opal and Jade crying. Amber raised her head, "I'm fine, so get back up there before one of you falls," Amber smiled. "I knew you would find me."

"You did? How did you know that?"

"Because I was supposed to call you when I got home, and since my phone is in the car, I couldn't. I knew you would figure out something was wrong."

I stopped climbing and looked at her. I couldn't stop the words that tumbled from my mouth and I didn't want to stop them. "Amber, I love you. I need to tell you I'm going to kill whoever pushed you off this cliff."

"You love me?"

Yes, sweetheart, I love you."

She had tears running down her cheeks, "I love you too."

"Can the two of you finish your conversation after you are safe on even ground?" Samuel demanded.

Amber chuckled. "That massive rock stopped the car just long enough for me to climb out the window. I know you love my curves but I wondered there for a moment if my curvy butt would fit through the window."

This time I chuckled. "Don't even think about changing anything. I love you the way you are." We had made it to the top, and I pulled her into my arms and kissed her. Then I felt Opal's, Jade's and Samuel's arms wrap around us. I figured I would have to get used to this because I wasn't going anywhere. When we stood on the road, I looked around for the woman and she wasn't there.

"Can I use someone's phone? I need to call this in?" Opal handed her cellphone to Amber and she made her call. She was back to business. I stared at her. She was the only woman I ever told "I love you" to. Now, what was I supposed to do?

"This better be good, it's five in the morning."

"Someone tried killing me last night." I listened as she talked to her chief. "I will need some handcuffs and a new car. My bag is still in my vehicle at the bottom of the cliff down there somewhere. It might have fallen out the window on the way down. I want paint chips from my vehicle. I'm through tiptoeing around these people. Someone tried to kill me, I want their ass locked up." She looked around. "I have a bumper. We can identify one vehicle," I heard her chuckle. "The license plate is on the bumper, that should tell us who owns it." She looked at me, smiled and walked towards me still talking on the phone and put her arms around me. She gazed into my eyes and kissed me while her boss was still talking.

"I'll see you when I get back to town." She looked at all of us. "Thank you for coming for me. I was afraid to climb up in case someone who wasn't nice saw me and finished what they sat out to do. Thank you, Donald, for helping him to find me."

"There's nothing to thank me for. I'm just happy you are safe. I'll do what I can to find out who did this to you."

"That would be a big help. But now that I know how serious these people are, I'm not sure that would be safe for you. You live with these people."

"I actually don't live here anymore. I live in South Carolina. I came back here for my father's funeral. That's why I'm packing what I want, then I'll be going back."

"Well, watch your back while you are here." He nodded in agreement and strolled over to his vehicle. Donald soon waved goodbye and drove off. We got in my vehicle and left. "We'll go by the hospital and have you checked out," I said as my hand rested on her thigh. She was sitting as close to me as she could get.

"That's not necessary. I'm fine."

"Well, then I'm taking you to see Ashley. She's married to Ryan. She's a doctor."

"Really, Jax, I'm fine. I don't need to see a doctor. I just want to go home and sleep."

"Okay, I'll let it go for now. You can sleep at my home."

"I doubt if I'll get any sleep at yours."

"I promise to behave," I leaned over and whispered into her ear.

I took Samuel and the girls home. They had already called Grandpa and told them we had found Amber. Then we drove to my home and I helped Amber with her shower. I helped her put one of my tee shirts on. Both of us got into bed and were asleep within minutes. I woke up a few hours later and made some coffee. I saw Jade sitting on my porch, so I poured her a cup and walked out to her. I'm glad I remembered to wear my sweats. I didn't have a shirt on.

"How come you're sitting out here? You should have come inside. I keep a spare key under the frog sitting right there."

"I'm sorry to intrude—"

I cut her off, "You can never intrude here. You are always welcome."

She smiled and continued, "I just wanted to be close to Amber. You know, she has always acted so strong, but she's no different than the rest of us. She must have been so scared. Those fuckers almost killed her." I watched as she gazed beyond the trees and then she looked at me. "I always wanted to help the person who was wrongly accused. It's getting harder and harder to tell if they are innocent. I've decided to quit my job, I don't want to defend bad people anymore. The only reason I became a public defender was that Opal and Amber were so angry that our father went to prison. I wanted to help innocent people. Now I just want to quit."

"Then quit, Jade. Don't spend your life doing something you don't want to do. You'll regret it forever. Do what makes you happy. What is it you want to do?"

"It is so far from what I am doing now, I'm sure you will think I am silly."

"I'm sure I won't." She stared off again. "Come on, tell me. I promise I won't think you are silly."

"I want to teach yoga," she said, still looking away.

"Then do it."

She gasped, "You really don't think that I am being immature? I mean, all those years of studying to throw it all away to become a yoga teacher."

"The best job anyone can do is the one that makes them happy. I think you should go for it."

After some silence between us, Jade looked at me as she smiled and said, "I will. I'm handing in my notice tomorrow. I'm going to do whatever I want, and if I don't like that, I will do something else."

"Good for you."

"I'm glad I came by to visit you, I used to run past this house all the time. I never knew who lived here."

"I bought this house two years ago when I decided to stay in one place. Are you happy your father is getting out of prison?"

"I'm not sure how I feel about it just yet. I mean, I don't know what will happen when he gets out. I don't want him disrupting our family... Is that horrible of me?"

"I don't think so. It's what you feel, so that's okay. You don't have family on your mother's side?"

"If we do, I haven't heard anything. We have always had Samuel with us. I don't remember him being anywhere else.

He's always taken care of us. Samuel is my father. I've known no other. I could never love another father any more than I love him. I don't want his feelings to get hurt. Do you know what I mean?"

"Yeah, I know. I'm sure everything will be fine. When your dad gets out, he'll be jumpy until he gets used to everything."

"I know. I see it every day. That's why I'm tired of being a public defender. I'm glad you love Amber. We all love you. I think Grandpa loves you more than any of us," she chuckled.

I laughed out loud. "I'm glad you stopped by. I'll have Amber call you when she wakes up. I better get back in there in case she has a bad dream."

"Bye Jax."

"See you soon."

I watched her as she ran down the path to their home. I had an uneasy feeling that something was about to happen. I wasn't sure what, but I knew it would happen. I crawled into bed next to Amber and pulled her into my arms. I loved her. I never thought I would fall in love. I knew I wanted her as mine but I felt like my heart swelled with my love for her. I would guard her with my life, and when I found out who tried to kill her, I would make them wish they had never been born.

11

JAX

"I can't believe you haven't been able to find anything."

"I've found plenty on Liam Penn. He's been in the service, and he went to college. He was never in trouble until he killed that man. I can't find anything on Grace Penn. It's like she never existed. I'm beginning to think she never existed before she got with Liam. I'm not sure if they were married even. I think you need to talk to Samuel and see what happened. You can't keep people safe if you don't know anything about them."

"Damn, that will mean Amber will find out I'm checking her family out, and I don't want her to know. I can't keep secrets from her."

"They all love you. I've known the family for a month, and I know they love you. They know you, Jax. Talk to them. Something isn't right. At first, I thought the father was in a witness protection program but I can find everything on him. I can't find who he married and I can't find where the girls were born. It's as if he was alone all this time. The only child who shows up is Ruby. I can find her birth record but only hers. I think you should talk to Samuel."

"You're right," I agreed, still a bit hesitant. "I'll talk to you later. I'm going to go talk to Samuel. I wouldn't say anything, but I have this damn feeling that something is about to hit the fan."

I pulled into the driveway, and all of them were home. I might as well get this over with. The door opened before I could knock and Amber threw her arms around me. She gave me a long hot kiss, then pulled me inside.

"Just in time for dinner."

"Great, you know I never turn down food."

I didn't say anything until dinner was over then I asked to speak to all of them. Axel had already left to play his games; he was allowed to play for an hour.

"What's the matter, Jax?"

"I've been having a sense of doom lately, like something is about to happen. You know that feeling that you get? And my feelings are right ninety percent of the time. The thing is, it concerns all of you."

"What do you mean? What kind of feeling? Maybe it's because our father is coming home," Amber said.

"No, I don't know how to tell you this, but I had Ryan check your father out. I thought it must be about him, but it's not. Your dad has never been in trouble except for that one time. So we checked your mom. We can't find anything on her, it's like she never existed. I can't find any birth certificates on you three, only on Ruby. I believe something is wrong, and I need to know what it is so I can help you."

What had I gotten myself into? Amber's face was red with anger. "I can't believe you did this. You checked our background out?" she screamed at the top of her lungs. She stood up, her teeth gritted, her stance strong, "Get out of this house. I don't want to talk to you right now. How dare you investigate us? What do you think we are, crooks? What, are you afraid that because our father is in prison, we are going to rob you? God, I knew better than to give my heart to you. You walked all over it without blinking an eye."

"Stop right there!" I bit back. She was so wrong. "I did not walk all over your heart. I gave you my heart also. I love you. When I have these feelings, I do something about it. I have saved lives with my feelings. Now," I turned to look at Samuel, "I need you to tell me what is wrong."

"Samuel, you don't have to say anything. Jax, leave right now. You are no longer welcome here."

"Samuel, tell him," Grandpa said.

"Tell him what?" Amber and Opal demanded.

Samuel took deep breaths. He looked scared. He took a big gulp of his drink before he said a word: "When Liam and I got out of the service, we met Grace. She was so beautiful and so broken down. She had three baby girls. Grace was hiding from her husband and his family. She knew if they found her, they would take the girls and kill her for daring to run away. She stayed with us on the farm. We bought the farm with the money we saved from the service.

"Grace and Liam fell in love—at least, Liam fell in love —and she became pregnant. I think she was already pregnant but I never voiced my thoughts out loud. She had the baby at a hospital in another state so she couldn't be tracked down. Everything was perfect until Grace got the fever of hunting for gems. She was obsessed with finding more and more. We tried telling her it was in her blood and she needed to quit before something happened. She didn't pay any attention to what we were saying.

"Grace got Jerry Elms to take her deep into the desert to find more gems. Liam was so scared that she would tell Jerry about your birth father and he would take you back to where he was. The next thing we knew, Grace had run off with Jerry. He killed her, and when we confronted him, he said he would tell your birth father where you were, so Liam killed him to save you girls. That's why there are no real birth certificate for any of you. I had them forged after your father went to prison. I needed to protect you. It was my responsibility."

"Who is our birth father?" Amber whispered.

"Gabriel Alvarez."

Amber's eyes were huge. "Gabriel Alvarez as in the mafia Gabriel? Our father is a mafia king?"

"Yes, that is what Grace told us. She changed all of your names. She liked Gems so much it got her killed. We think Liam is Ruby's dad."

Amber was shaking, I could feel her beside me. I put my arm around her and pulled her up next to me. "Was there something wrong with our mother mentally? What were our names before she changed them?"

"I have everything written down, I'll get it, and you can look at it. She wasn't mentally damaged, or maybe she was. She would have deep depression moods. I always thought she fried her brain somewhat from drugs, I don't know. I know that we were told if he ever found you, he would kill all of you."

Opal was pacing back and forth, wringing her hands. "Wait, you're telling us that our drugged-out mother told you and Liam this story about a mafia king and you two believed her? She fucked up both of your lives because you two thought a mafia lord would come and take us away? Did you think he wouldn't kill us if we were his daughters? Was Grace her real name?"

"I don't know," Samuel said, shaking his head. "Now it sounds stupid when I say it out loud but when you became pregnant, I knew you would need a hospital and they would want all of your information, I panicked and we moved here."

Opal looked at Samuel, shaking her head. "I can't believe this is happening. Was it true about you being stollen? Is anything we've known the truth?"

"Yes, that's true. The only thing I kept from you is about what Grace told us."

"You also left out the fact that Liam wasn't our father."

Amber looked at Samuel, and I thought she might cry. "Why didn't you tell us? We wouldn't have rushed off to find him. We love you and Grandpa. I have to know if this is the truth." She turned and looked at me. "Is there any way we can find out if this is true?"

"I'll talk to Ryan. Wouldn't you think he would have done a blood test and checked it in the DNA files? If he were your father, he would know how to find you. This isn't what I was expecting to hear. I thought your mom was in the witness protection program or something. We have to be careful on how to go about this, I don't want anyone getting on the computer and checking him out. They have things that can show who's been looking at your profile."

Amber looked at me and wiped a tear away. "I'm sorry I shouted at you."

"Sweetheart, I promise I wouldn't have done any snooping if I didn't feel like something was off. If this man is your father, he can never know where you are. I don't think Samuel would be safe because he hid you. We don't want him to know anything about Axel."

"He wouldn't be able to find us in the DNA files because we've never given a sample.

Samuel told us never to let anyone take a sample of our blood. I'm worried about you thinking something was going to happen, what should we do?"

"Don't do anything, I'll find out what's going on. I'll let all of you know what I learn. Quite frankly, I don't think your mother was telling the truth about any of this. I would love to know her real name." I looked over at Samuel. "Do you believe she was telling the truth?"

"I should have paid more attention but I had my own problems back then and Liam was only nineteen. I don't know what's true and what isn't."

I frowned, looking at him. "I thought he was in the service."

"He was, but was hurt while in training. He was shot and was discharged after a year. He got some money, so when I got out, we bought the farm. It was right after that we found Grace hiding with you girls."

"Where did you find her hiding?" Jade asked.

"She was behind the garbage bin in Vegas. We thought we would treat ourselves because we were doing good selling our fruit and vegetables at our stand. We went to Vegas for the weekend. Liam heard one of you crying and he investigated where it was coming from. After Grace told us about her hiding with you girls, Liam brought all of you home with us."

Jade shook her head, "She sounds like any other druggy I've come in contact with being a public defender. I'm going to visit Liam. I have to know if he knows something he never told you."

"I'm going with you, Amber and Opal said simultaneously."

"I don't know if that's a good idea," Samuel said, looking at each sister.

"Are you kidding me? Liam was barely an adult when our mother roped him into her lies and he has lost his entire life because of it. How old was I at that time?"

"You were two, Amber was three and Opal was four. I knew that because Opal told us how old you three were."

"Did we ever mention our father?"

"At first you cried for your father all the time. You missed him. I remember talking to Liam about that, but he was so in love he wouldn't listen to what I had to say. Eventually, I quit asking."

"So I was five when Liam went to prison, he was twenty-one. He was a child. You two were making a dream come true and then you met Grace. I'm sorry for everything that's happened to you and Liam. I'm ashamed to be the daughter of Grace. I need to think, I'm going for a walk."

I stood up to go with her, and she looked at me shaking her head, "I need to be with my sisters." I watched as all three of them walked out the door.

AMBER

We had walked about two miles when I finally said something. "I don't like what's going on in my head!" I screamed. I couldn't help it. "She used that nineteen-year-old boy who fell deeply in love with her. And she destroyed his life and Samuel's. I think she took us from our father, why else would we cry for him? We wanted our father. We have to work together on this." I don't believe he is Gabriel Alvarez. We have no Hispanic blood in us. She lied about that too. Our eyes are light, our skin is light. Ruby is the only one with black hair, and that's because Liam is probably her father."

"I agree. I'm going to check for missing children. I feel in my heart we were taken from our father. I can feel him. He loved us. I remember his face. He was always smiling," Opal said, wiping a tear off her cheek. "We would never have known anything if Jax hadn't felt something was off. How come we never felt it? We never questioned anything about Samuel raising us. We are all well-educated women, what is wrong with us? Jax knew us for a week when he felt something was off."

I looked at my sisters. "Why don't we go to my office and see what we can find out?"

We walked back home. Jax had already left. We told Samuel we were going shopping. We didn't want to get involved in a discussion if we didn't know it to be true. We looked back to the year Samuel met Grace. We checked the United States. It took one minute. We saw our dad holding us and a picture of our mother, who stole us from him. Opal ran her fingers down the screen, "Daddy," she whispered. We both remembered him and tears fell unchecked down our cheeks. He was no mafia guy; he was our father who loved us and we loved him. We scrolled through the years, and he never stopped looking for us. He went all over the United States hunting for us.

"We have to go to him," Opal said. We made reservations that day, we would be leaving the following morning. We didn't want to hurt Samuel but we wanted to see our dad. Jade didn't remember him but she wanted to know the truth.

When I got home, I called Jax and told him everything. "Our mother lied. She must have been a horrible woman. She fucked up Liam and Samuel's lives. I'm so ashamed because I was related to her. We are leaving in the morning to visit our father. We don't want to call him. I don't know why but that's what we agreed on."

"Where does he live?"

"In Montana. He lives on a ranch. Opal and I remember the horses. He would set us in front of him on the horse and take us with him. There was someone else also, I think he was our uncle."

"I'm going with you."

"Good, I was hoping you would say that; I got you an airplane ticket. Are you home?"

"Yes."

"I'll be there in two minutes."

He met me half way and our conversation continued from there. "Opal remembers everything about him, I only remember a few things. I remember he told us bedtime stories. He had complete custody of us because Jill was flighty. She was considered dangerous to us because she was doing drugs."

"So her name wasn't Grace? What did Samuel say about it?"

"He feels awful that he believed her. Liam gets out on the tenth of next month. We aren't going to tell Ruby about all of this until Jade goes over there next week."

"I'm so shocked. Still, I can't believe I never thought to question Samuel about the other family we might have had. I wonder why that was."

"Because you were happy, you didn't have to worry about someone not loving you because Samuel and Grandpa loved you. Are you hungry?"

"No, I want you to hold me. I want to feel safe. Make love to me."

He picked me up and carried me to the bed. I laughed at how fast he had us undressed. Jax pulled me under him, gazed into my eyes and said, "I love you so much, I want you to be happy." He kissed me, and my mind only had thoughts of him. Everything else vanished from my thoughts. All I could think of was Jax and what he was doing to me. I cried out as his hand slipped down between my legs. I held my breath as his two fingers pushed inside me. Now my breathing was uneven, I reached down and wrapped my hand around his stiff erection.

"Unless you want me to climax early, you'll drop that." I

chuckled as I squeezed harder. We made sweaty, hot, sexy love for the rest of the afternoon.

I was lying next to him when I heard his stomach growl and giggled. "I'll make you an omelet." I got up and took a quick shower.

"What is your father's name?" Jax asked when I came back into the room.

"Gabe Martin, our names are the same except for our last name, so I'm Amber Martin."

"Nice to know you, Amber Martin," he said, coming up behind me and wrapping his arms around me. He kissed my neck. "I love you no matter what your name is."

"I love you so much," I said, turning in his arms and kissing him. "I'm so glad you're coming with us."

"OH, my God, I'm so nervous. What if he's not home?" Jade said for the hundredth time. What if he has a heart attack or something. Jax, how did you get his address? Never mind. I know I've asked that a hundred times already. She burst into tears. I watched as Jax pulled her into his arms.

"Jade, it's going to be okay, stop worrying. He still has his daughters and now you will make him so happy. Come on, let's go meet your father."

We rented an SUV and drove for an hour, then there was a huge sign that said Martin Ranch. Jax drove down the long driveway and stopped in front of the large home. All three of us girls were crying. Jax got out when a man rode up on a horse.

"Can I help you?"

"We're looking for Gabe Martin."

"That's me."

Opal flew out of the vehicle as the man got off his horse. Then I stepped out, and so did Jade, still crying uncontrollably. I turned when another man stepped out of the house. Our father stumbled, then he straightened.

"Daddy," Opal cried, running to him. He wrapped his arms around her. He was crying right along with her, then he looked at me and I ran into his arms. Jade stood there and looked at the man who had come from the house.

"Uncle," he ran to her and pulled her into his arms.

"How can you remember me, squirt?" his cheeks were bathing in his tears.

"I don't know," she answered.

Axel stood next to Jax until Opal pulled him into her arms with our dad.

"Daddy, this is my son, Axel."

"My grandson," he sobbed, "I have a grandson. I can't believe this is happening, my dream has come true." He held Axel tight as the both of them cried. It was hard to believe this was happening, that we were reunited with our father.

It was loud and crazy before everyone settled down enough for us to talk. "How did you find me? Tell me everything," my dad said, wiping his eyes. "I never thought I would see you three again. Your uncle, Chase, and I have looked everywhere..." his voice was breaking. My uncle patted his back. "I can't believe you are here in front of me right now." He wiped his eyes, "Come, come inside and let's talk. I want to know everything about you." Then he spotted Jax. "I'm sorry, what's your name?"

"Jax Black, I'm with Amber."

"Jax, come inside, please."

I took Jax's hand, mine was shaking so much I needed to get through this. I had to convince my dad that Samuel and

Liam believed what our mother told them. They thought they were protecting us. We talked until midnight, Marie the housekeeper, fixed dinner while we visited. My dad remarried and had a ten-year-old son. They were away visiting her family. I was anxious to meet them.

Chase had his own home on the property spread out over one thousand acres. He had four kids that were all grown, two worked on the ranch and two lived on other ranches nearby. They were nice guys. I felt comfortable with Gabe, I was up early and he already had the coffee on. He poured us a cup, and we sat down at the large island.

"Thank you for investigating us. I wouldn't have a chance ever of seeing my girls again. I still don't understand why Samuel wouldn't have checked something out, Liam was fooled just like me. The only difference is that he was so young and spent twenty years in a physical prison. I was a grown man who wanted to kill my ex-wife for stealing my girls and I remained trapped in my mind until now. I won't press charges against Samuel, he loves the girls. I mean, his own life was shit. Besides, one of my daughters is the district attorney and one is a homicide detective. Jade stopped being a lawyer, which she never enjoyed, to own a yoga studio. I am very blessed." He spoke in a pensive tone.

"Samuel and Grandpa love these girls like they were

their father and grandfather. They have had a good life. Then there is Ruby, she is Liam's daughter, it would be hard to press charges with her being involved. You know this is the first time the girls have been apart? They have all lived in the same house forever. Ruby has black hair but she looks like her sisters. But then your hair is black, is there any way she could be your daughter?"

I could see his face turning red and waited for him to speak. "Yes, there is a chance, Jill had me thinking she changed and we slept together the night before she took the girls. I'll do a DNA test to see if she is mine. Tell me about her."

"I don't know a lot. Ruby teaches hand-to-hand combat for the government. She is a private investigator and not for married couples. She investigates crooked politicians among other things. Amber told me she's deadly, so don't make her angry at you. Samuel taught the girls how to fight. Ruby has lots of belts in martial arts as well. What do you think about what Liam and Samuel were told?"

Gabe shook his head, he looked disgusted with life in general. I knew it was Jill who disgusted him. "Let me tell you something, the best thing that could have happened to the girls was their mother dying. Jill was nothing but trouble. It doesn't surprise me at all that she messed up those boys' lives, she almost destroyed my family's life. Chase finally sat me down and told me everything she'd been doing. She got hooked on drugs and I put her in rehab a few times. I had already had sole custody of the girls. I didn't want her anywhere around them. I got her a place in town to live so she could visit them when she was sober again. I mean, girls need their mothers, so I was willing to help her sort herself out. The last time she was in rehab, I truly believed she had changed until she ran off with my children.

I think she had help. She was always talking on the phone to drug users. Jill claimed it was part of her rehab to speak to other drug addicts," he shrugged. "I don't even want to keep talking about her. I'm going to see if the girls have a photo of Ruby."

"She knows they are visiting you." That's when we heard a car door slam shut. We opened the front door when Ruby raised her hand to knock.

She stared at Gabe for a moment, then she threw her arms around him. "I knew you were my father as soon as I saw a photo of you. Two years ago, I did a DNA test and knew Liam wasn't my dad. I didn't say anything because I didn't want to hurt Samuel or Grandpa."

Gabe threw back his head and laughed out loud. "What's so funny?" Amber said coming around the corner. "Ruby, what are you doing here? I missed you so much." They hugged and then Amber looked from her dad and then back to Ruby a few times. "Is Gabe your dad?"

"Yes, how did you guess?"

"I wondered about it after meeting him. Plus, you have the same eye color as our uncle."

"Do we have an uncle?" Ruby asked, stepping into the house. Gabe and I followed, smiling. They were still talking when the others walked into the kitchen.

"Ruby, what are you doing here? We haven't had a chance to tell you what was going on."

"Samuel told me. He said he looked at a photo of Gabe and thought he might be my dad. I've known for two years Liam wasn't my father. I didn't want to hurt anyone because I knew we weren't supposed to have any tests done. You know me, I have to investigate things. I didn't check to see who my dad was, I am glad it's Gabe. We have the same father. I can't stay long; I have to get back to Scotland. But I can stay a couple of days. What will happen to Liam?"

Amber shook her head and laughed. "You just spoke a mile per minute!" The other sisters laughed. "I guess that is up to him. We were little girls tricked by a woman I wish wasn't our mother. Let's all go to the kitchen and I'll make us breakfast."

We heard the front door open and voices. "We are in the kitchen," Gabe called out.

Chase and four others walked in. Amber took out more eggs, we heard a car door slam and she took out more, then she took out the bacon and Opal started making up the dough for biscuits. "Is this..." Chase asked, hugging Ruby.

"So you have four daughters," Garret said—he was one of Chase's sons.

"How can you tell besides the black hair?" Gabe asked.

"She has mine and Dad's gray eyes. See the dimple in her chin," he pointed to his chin. "She's definitely a Martin."

Ruby's chin wobbled and Garret put his arm around her. We spent an entire week there before we went back home. The girls missed Samuel and Grandpa. The biggest surprise to all of us was that Ruby handed in her notice and was now moving to Montana to live. I dropped the sisters off at their house and then I headed home. I had to leave on a rescue mission the following morning. I was sound asleep when I felt a hand wrap around me in the middle of the night. "What are you doing out this late at night?"

"I missed you not being near me and I couldn't sleep, so I ran over here in my pajamas."

"Well, you know we can't have that. No pajamas are allowed in our bed."

"I know, I already took them off. How long are you going to be gone?"

"I don't know. We never know how long it takes us. Sometimes we are back in a few days and sometimes a few weeks. Everything depends on where they are and how many."

"I'm going to miss you."

"I'll miss you too. I pulled Amber under me and nibbled her ear, and then my lips made their way down her soft body. There wasn't a spot on her I didn't taste. I made sure she would remember this night for a long time. I didn't want to leave her with so much stuff going on in her life but I had to. I kissed her again as we said goodbye.

"Jax, take care of yourself. I love you and I want you to come back to me."

"I will, sweetheart, and you take care of yourself. You are the only love for me." I pulled her into my arms, "I won't be able to call you while I'm over there but as soon as we get back on the plane, I'll call, I promise."

AMBER

Liam was out of prison and on his way to Maine. He knew the truth, so we were surprised he was coming here. Samuel wanted to tell us something, I could tell by how he paced back and forth in the kitchen. "Samuel, spit it out. I know you have something to say, what is it?"

"I don't understand why Liam is coming here, he knows the truth. He isn't related to any of you. We haven't seen him in so many years, why is he coming here?"

"Do you think he might start some trouble?"

"I don't know why else he's coming. I don't want you girls to be alone with him. He's pissed off because he blames your mother for everything, I don't know what he'll do. He's angry at me because I told him not to come here. I explained that it was no use coming here because there was no family here for him."

"I wondered about that myself. Axel and Opal will be in Montana and Ruby will be there too. We need to tell Jade. I don't want him around her. She looks the most like our mother. Maybe she and Grandpa can go to Montana."

"I'm not sure your grandpa will want to do that."

"Yes, I will," Grandpa said, walking into the kitchen. "I already told Jade that I wanted to go to Montana, we are leaving in an hour. I made reservations, I think you also need to leave, Amber. I have a bad feeling about him coming here. He got himself in this mess but he'll want to blame you girls."

"Grandpa, I'm a homicide detective, I can handle Liam. I will not leave. I'm staying here with Samuel. We'll meet with Liam and see what he has to say. I'm sure everything will be okay. He must be devastated knowing the family he thought he had is no longer his family. He killed a man because he thought it would keep the children safe, and we've never been in danger. She lied to him, we didn't. He was a child. I hate that she was my mother but we are not to blame for everything she did, and I won't let anyone blame my sisters or me. I won't run, afraid to look behind me for the rest of our lives. I'm making my stand right here right now, I will tell Jade goodbye, and then I have to go to work."

I WORRIED the entire day about Samuel being home alone, so I left work early. Jax had been gone for two weeks and I missed him so much. I pulled into the driveway and saw Samuel walking with a man, I knew it was Liam. I got out of the car and stopped. I saw a gun in Liam's hand pointed at Samuel's back. I called out to him and his attention focused on me.

"Liam, you don't want to do this, why have you got a gun on Samuel? He didn't do anything wrong."

"Let me guess, Amber the cop. He could have made me leave Grace alone."

"Her name was Jill, and he couldn't make you do anything you didn't want to do."

"I'm not Ruby's father, that was all I lived for, my Ruby." He was crying.

"Liam, you are only forty-two, you can still have children. You're young, don't do this. Don't throw the rest of your life away. She's not worth it. She's taken enough from you."

"You look just like her, are you like her? Do you drive men insane with your lies?"

My eyes went to Samuel, I knew he was going to do something stupid. I started to raise my hand when the bullet hit me in the chest. My gun went off and I shot Liam. It was all so senseless. My sight was turning black when I fell to the ground. I heard Samuel screaming my name. I heard sirens but they seemed so far away. *Jax, Jax, I'm so sorry. I didn't mean to die, please believe me. I love you!*

"It's okay, sweetheart. Amber, help is here, please hang on, honey. Please don't die."

"Jax, tell Jax I love him."

"You'll tell him yourself, sweetheart."

"Fuck, what the hell happened to Amber?" Jeff asked, jumping out of his vehicle.

"That guy there shot her, his name is Liam Penn. He just got out of prison. He was in there for murder, I'm going to the hospital, I believe he's dead."

I couldn't wait to see Amber. We stopped so I could buy her flowers and chocolates. I may have eaten a few of them. I was humming under my breath when Ryan pulled into their driveway. What I saw scared the crap out of me. We jumped out of his vehicle when I saw Samuel crying. I ran to the ambulance and what I was afraid of came true. Amber was in the back, covered in blood. Angel jumped in the back and kicked the EMT out. "What happened?" I asked the EMT, who was still in shock. I didn't think either of them had seen anything like this.

"She was shot in the chest, there is a dead man out there, I'm assuming she shot him."

"How bad is it?" I asked Angel.

"It isn't good, let's get the hell out of here."

I jumped in the driver's seat and Samuel jumped in the passenger seat. "You can ride with Ryan in the truck," I shouted to the driver. More police pulled into the driveway.

I looked at Samuel, "Was that Liam?"

"Yeah, he came to kill the girls. He blamed them for him going to prison, I almost had him out of there, I was going to take him away and kill him if I could but Amber came home early."

"Where are the others?"

"They are all in Montana, Amber wouldn't leave."

"Jax, what is going on? Just get us to the hospital, fast."

I drove so fast that I had three cop cars following me. I pulled into the emergency lane at the hospital, the police jumped out at the same time we did. "This is Detective Penn, she's been shot, so get the fuck out of my way."

We rushed her into the emergency entrance and Angel made me stay behind as they wheeled her to the operation room. It seemed like forever that Samuel and I sat in the waiting room. My friends and my brother and his wife came to sit with us. I looked over at Samuel, and his chin started to wobble, I reached over and squeezed his hand. "She's going to be okay. We have to think positively."

"I know, I'm just so scared."

"I know, I am..." I didn't get to finish my sentence. A nurse ran in and shouted for me to follow her. She threw me a mask and I put it on. I saw my sweetheart lying on the table, blood was everywhere.

"Jax, yell at her, tell her to live. I'm losing her."

"No!" I shouted. I dropped the mask. "Amber, you listen to me, if you don't fight to stay with me, I will never forgive you. Please, sweetheart, fight with all you have, don't let this take you from me. I love you, baby. Please don't give up." I kissed her mouth, and I could feel her lips were cold. It sent a shock I'd never experienced before straight through me. Tears came down my face instantly, I couldn't hold them back. "Please don't do this, Amber. You don't get to leave me. You promised me you would take care of yourself." My tears dropped on her cheek but I didn't care who saw it.

I begged her and cried on her until Angel said, "She's back."

My forehead leaned against hers as I kept on talking. I told her what we were going to do in the future. "First, we are getting married, and you are not leaving my bed, I'm keeping you where I know you are safe."

"Okay, I'm going to finish up here, you can go back to the waiting room."

"No, I'm staying right here, do what you have to do." One of the nurses handed me a napkin and I wiped my eyes. Finally, when everything was okay, I went back to the waiting room and told everybody Amber was going to make it. Samuel and I walked together to the ICU. I was sleeping in a chair when I heard whispering. I opened my eyes and all of Amber's family was there, Amber still hadn't woken up. I hugged all of them. I'll admit I may have cried some more with her sisters. Samuel came in and gave me some hot coffee.

"All of you cannot be in here, two guests at a time. Pick two and the rest will have to wait in the waiting room."

"I'm not leaving, so two more can stay then you can switch. You can pick which ones are visiting with Amber first."

"You misunderstood me sir, only two at a time are allowed in here."

"I'm not leaving, Amber has two fathers and a Grandpa here and three sisters. If you have a problem, take it up with Dr. Angel Davis. He told me I could stay with Amber, but I would remain even if he hadn't told me."

"And a brother."

I looked around, Gabe, a woman and a boy stood there.

"And a mother," the woman said.

Damn, if water didn't try to overflow from my eyes again.

"Yes, and a brother and a mother." I took tissues from the holder and handed them to Jade.

"You need to keep these," Jade said with her arm still around me.

"We'll do it this way, Samuel and Grandpa can visit for ten minutes, then Gabe, Reese, and Luke, her little brother. She'll want to hear him talking to her. Is that alright with you girls?" I heard a chuckle and looked over at Amber. She was smiling. "Sweetheart, thank you for living. Damn it, my allergies are so bad!" I said as I rushed over to her and wiped my eyes before kissing her forehead. "Look who came to visit you. Everyone is here." I knew she was thinking about Liam, I saw the tears falling.

"Did I kill him?"

"You had no choice." Samuel stepped up next to the bed and kissed her forehead.

"If you hadn't done what you did, he would kill all of you girls. He started doing drugs in prison, it made him crazy. You did nothing wrong."

"I know. I hate that I'm related to the woman that caused all of this. Liam didn't deserve to be roped into her web of lies. She ruined a child's life."

"Amber, he shot you, don't forget that. He came to our house to kill, nothing else. Now, rest and stop thinking of Liam, he wasn't the same person and it wasn't your fault, none of it."

I kissed her. "I love you, and I almost lost you. I'm going to call Angel and tell him you are awake."

Her eyes landed on the boy and she smiled. "So you are my little brother, I've always wanted a brother, and you look like Ruby."

"I know we look alike. Everyone says so. She is teaching

me how to fight, she said she would teach me how to street fight in case I ever needed to use it."

Ruby laughed out loud. "That was supposed to be our secret."

"I know, but I already told Dad, so I thought I would tell Amber. She's my sister too."

"That she is," Ruby said, ruffling his hair.

"Do you like having sisters?" Amber asked him.

"Yeah, I love my sisters, and Jake said all of you were hot."

Amber grinned. "Who's Jake?"

"He has a ranch near ours. I heard him tell Uncle Chase, and Uncle Chase told him not to worry about how hot you girls were. My mom said she would bring some fans in the house when I told her what Jake said." Everyone chuckled.

"Luke, I love having you for my brother." She fell asleep before saying another word. There was a long sigh of relief that went around the room.

"Is she dead?" Luke asked, crying.

"No, she's sleeping," Gabe said, smiling. "How about all of us go out for lunch?"

"I'll stay here and wait for Angel, you all go."

"We'll bring you something back."

"Okay, thank you."

I looked at the door and Emily stood there, looking at everyone. I saw her mentally counting the people. She always did that. It's how she makes sure to cook enough food. "I have lunch cooking for everyone, we will all go to my house. I knew you wouldn't come, Jax, so I brought you something to eat."

I walked over and kissed her cheek. "Thank you." I looked at the girls, "You all remember Emily."

"Yes," Samuel said. "There are too many of us to feed."

"Nonsense, I've got it warming in the oven, I'm a chef, I love cooking. If you can handle the noise the kids make at mealtime, then please follow me." I watched as all of them followed Emily out the door.

"Good, now we are alone," Amber whispered from the bed.

"This is the way I like it, but your family will be back after they finish lunch."

"Hello, am I interrupting anything?" Angel said with a massive grin on his face.

"Yes, we wanted to be alone before the family members get back from lunch with Emily."

"I'm on my way there right now, I'll tell them they can see her tomorrow. I'll have Samuel get some clean clothes from your house, and you can shower in an empty room somewhere. I'm glad to see you are awake, how do you feel?"

"Sore, thank you for saving my life."

"You're welcome. I'm sorry you had to kill someone you knew and loved. That is so hard. I had to do that once, it messed me up for a while. Always remember this, you didn't have a choice, he did."

"I watched as Amber nodded her head, then she closed her eyes and went back to sleep.

"She's a fighter, she'll live until she's an old lady but you should talk to her about taking on another job. I didn't say anything, I wanted to wait until I was sure." Angel looked at me and smiled, "Amber is pregnant."

"What? Oh Lord, I'm going to have a baby." I bent my head and cried. "He could have killed both of them," I let out as the realization hit me. My anger started to boil instantly. He was lucky to be dead already because I would have killed him with my bare hands.

"But he didn't, so now all you need to do is talk her into a safe job where she can have the baby with her."

"Yes, I'll think of something. Thank you, you seem to always be in the right place at the right time. I'm so happy to call you brother."

"I have to go out of town for a few days, Ashley will take over for me. We all know she's a damn good doctor."

"Thanks, now I can't wait for Amber to wake up so I can tell her about the baby."

16

JAX

I paced back and forth in front of the window, anxious one moment in the next my anxiety would shoot up. I was trying to think about how I would tell Amber about the baby. I've never discussed children with her. She hadn't even moved in with me. I mean, she was at my house almost every night. I wanted her there every night. I didn't want her to go back with Samuel, I wanted her to marry me. Would she think I only wanted to marry her because of the baby?

"What has you so anxious, did something happen?" Samuel asked.

He handed me some clothes and I looked at him, "No, nothing is wrong with Amber. I have some news, Angel told me," I hesitated to tell him, and then I decided just to say it. I knew I had a massive grin on my face, I pulled him near the window, "we are having a baby."

"What? Oh my God! What if he had shot lower."

"Come and sit down. He didn't shoot lower and that's a good thing. You're going to be a grandpa again."

"Yes, I am happy. Does Amber know?"

"No, I'll tell her when she wakes up. Can you stay here while I shower?"

"Yes, go ahead. If she wakes up before you get back, I won't say a word."

I nodded and went down three doors and showered. When I got back to the room, Amber was awake, and she and Samuel were talking. Amber was trying to assure him she was okay.

When she saw me, she smiled. "Hi, sweetheart."

"Hey, you know you don't have to stay with me?"

"I want to stay with you. I want to be where you are for the rest of my life. You know how much I love you, don't think you're going to send me home. I'll park my butt outside the door right now."

"I love you too."

"Amber, I'm going to ask you something, I want you to think about it for a moment but always remember I love you. Will you marry me? I know I never want to be without you in my life."

"Yes."

"Yes, you will?"

"Yes."

"You heard her, Samuel; she can't take it back. You are a witness."

Samuel laughed at that.

"I don't want to take it back. I want to marry you and I want to be with you forever."

"Congratulations you two," Samuel said.

"Sweetheart, I have fantastic news; we're having a baby!" I wasn't sure she heard me. "Say something."

"I'm pregnant?" Amber started hyperventilating. "He could have killed my baby. I could have killed my baby." She began to cry, so Samuel called her sisters to come and talk to her. I could not calm her down. I called Ashley when Amber spaced out. It was like she went into herself. It took Ashley ten minutes to get there. Nothing I said would get through to her.

"She's in shock but she'll be fine. Back up, Jax, so I can check her out. Amber, look at me." Ashley called a nurse in and ordered medication for Amber.

"What was that for?"

"It's to calm her down, tell me what happened?"

"I asked her to marry me, and she said yes then I told her we were having a baby. She said the baby could have been killed, and it would have been her fault. I tried to tell her the only person at fault here was Liam but I couldn't get through to her. What is wrong with her? Do something."

Ashley looked at me. "Go sit down before I have you kicked out of here."

Samuel pulled me away, and then her sisters walked into the room.

"What happened to her?" Opal demanded.

"I told her we were having a baby and she became upset. She said she could have killed her baby."

"I could have killed my baby, all of you in here know that. I left work early because I was afraid Liam would hurt Samuel and I got shot. Oh my God, my baby could have died."

"Amber, you're having a baby?"

The girls gathered around her while I stood back and watched them cry. I even saw Ashley wipe a tear away, she was ready to pop. She and Ryan were expecting in a few weeks. Ashley is a true hero—she even has a medal to prove it. I saw her in action in Ukraine, saving lives.

Finally, Amber looked at me with squinted eyes, "Is this why you asked me to marry you."

"You know that's not why I asked. I want to marry you because I love you. When you leave here, you are coming home with me. Samuel and your sisters can visit you there, that will now be our home. You can do anything you want to it."

"All I'll want to do is decorate the baby's room. I'll hand in my notice as soon as I can. I'm staying home with my baby. Samuel, do you think you can help decorate your grandbaby's room?"

"I would love to help you with that. I'll paint it. I don't want you around any paint while you're pregnant." All of a sudden Samuel looked shy, as if he wanted to say something but was worried about what we'd think. Then he steadied himself and said sternly, too sternly at that, "While I got all of you here, I want you to know I've been dating a woman and I'm going to have her over for dinner one night when we are all together."

They were all happy for Samuel. I looked at Amber, "I'm tired, can I squeeze in next to you?"

"Yes, we'll both take a nap."

We went to sleep as the family chattered away about the baby. No one wanted to mention Liam, at least not when others were around. I thought Samuel may have known he was doing drugs. Most people in prison constantly wanted someone to fill an order or put money on their books.

17

AMBER

That man made me so angry he was treating me like I had broken all my limbs. "Jax, I can do something, I'm not helpless."

"That's not what Angel said. He said you couldn't pick anything up, a basket of clothes is not light. Sit down, I'll wash the clothes."

"Why don't you go shopping for the baby? She's going to need sweet things for her walls."

"You can't get rid of me that easily. Besides, how do you know our baby is a girl?"

"I don't know, I just feel that she's a girl. Would you mind if we have a girl?"

"Sweetheart, I don't care if we have ten baby girls, I will love them all the same."

"I knew you would say that. That's why I love you so much. I'm not sure about ten kids, but we'll have at least five, maybe six." I smiled at the look on his face. This was fun, I could tease Jax and enjoy it because he was acting like a watchdog. Then he picked me up and sat me on his lap.

"You make me so happy. I want a dozen baby's with you."

"God, I love you," I said as I pulled his tee-shirt over his head.

"No, we are not making love, you are not ready for me to make love to you."

"Sure I am."

"Angel said he would kick my ass if I made love to you before your body is healed."

"My body is ready, screw what Angel says. He's probably laughing because he told you that. Okay, what if we do it slowly?"

"You don't know slow sweetheart. Why do you think I've been keeping my hands to myself?" he asked. His body was saying something his lips weren't. His hands roamed under my top and he had my bra unhooked in a snap. I let my lips touch his, then I threw my leg across him and scooted closer to his stiff erection.

"Sweetheart, you're killing me," he picked me up and carried me to the bed where he made slow hot sexy love to me.

"That was so good. I didn't know it could be like that going so slow. Let's do it again." I knew I would get my way. I went to sleep after the third time. When I got up, the laundry was finished, and dinner was on the stove.

"Yummy, what are you making?"

"Samuel made it, he brought it over. All I had to do was heat it. I like living near to your family, I might gain a few pounds but it's worth it. Ruby is back, she said she missed all of you and it would take time for her to get used to living far away. So she may just stay around here. And she can visit your dad and the Montana family."

"I'm confused, is Ruby going to move to Montana? Or is she coming back here to stay?"

"I don't think she knows yet."

"Poor Ruby, I hope she stays here. She thought Liam was her father her entire life. He thought he was her father too. He killed that man to save us girls. At least he thought he did. I imagine that was what got him through prison for these twenty years, knowing he had a family to come home to."

"Sweetheart, he shot you. He was there to kill all of you girls and Samuel."

"I know that, but I wrote to him all the time. It will take time for me to come to terms with Liam, the killer, and Liam the father. I would have never known about our birth father if you hadn't investigated us."

"Are you thanking me?" Jax teased, pulling me into his arms.

"Yes, I am."

"Good," he kissed my lips softly. "Are we ready to set a date for our wedding?"

"I haven't had time to think about our wedding day, do you mind if we hold off on that for a while? I swear I feel like I've been running a marathon. I want to have time to think of the baby right now."

"As long as you know we are getting married, I don't mind."

"I know, I promise it'll be soon."

"Samuel said he'll be here to paint the baby's room this weekend, I think he wants you to go to the hardware store with him."

"Okay, can you come with us? I've been to the hardware store with Samuel, he gets in the tool department and never leaves. I wonder how far along I must be, at least three months pregnant. So that still gives us time to buy baby furniture. I know this sounds crazy, but I'm so excited about having a baby, I could just cry every time I think about it."

"If it sounds crazy, then I'm crazy right along with you. We will be great parents."

"Yes, we will. For some reason, I get weepy thinking about our baby."

"That's okay, sweetheart, you can get as weepy as you want."

"I'm not a weepy kind of person." Jax threw back his head and laughed. "That's for damn sure you are not a weepy person."

"Ruby, I don't know, is it safe?"

"If it were any safer, you would have to wrap bubble wrap around it, this is the perfect baby bed. Amber, this is the only store left. Now you have seen every baby bed there is to see. You have photos on your phone to look at whenever you want, decide this week. I've been shopping with you six times for a baby bed."

I did buy more baby clothes, but I couldn't decide what furniture. The walls were painted a soft yellow. When we got home, Ruby came in to have a glass of tea. I heard talking down the hall and wondered who was with Jax. Ruby and I walked down the hall to the baby's room and Jax and Trey were there putting baby furniture together. The dresser and changing table were ready for the baby and the bed was almost complete.

"Jax, this is beautiful, where did you get it?"

"I got it at Baby's Are Us, I knew you were having difficulty deciding, so I went yesterday and picked it out."

"That cream color is perfect, I love it. I just love it."

"That's the same one we looked at," Ruby said.

"Are you sure? I don't think the color was the same."

"That's because I asked for this color, I thought you would rather have this color," Jax said. "You told me you didn't want white, brown, or yellow. I knew you would like this one.

"This color makes all the difference, thank you. Trey, how are you doing?"

"I'm good, how are you doing? Ruby, how are you? So are you staying here in Maine?"

"I'm good. I have to decide what I want to do. I gave notice and I've decided to start a security business. I know a lot of people, so I'm trying to think of a name. I don't want my customers to have any doubt that I can do my job."

"This is wonderful, I'm so happy for you. I mean, you ran the security company you just left. That means you will be here when our baby is born."

"Yes, I don't want to leave. I like being here with my sisters, Samuel, and Grandpa." She looked at Trey, "If you know anyone looking to get into the business, please send them my way. I need people who know what they are doing. I prefer someone who knows how to fight, I don't want to have to train anyone in that regard. I'm hoping Samuel will become my partner, I'm going to ask him tonight."

I threw my arms around Ruby. I knew this would be perfect for Samuel. "That is a fantastic idea, I'm sure he will say yes. We'll let you two finish what you are doing, I have some baby clothes to wash."

I heard him ask Jax how far along I was. Jax chuckled, "Three months."

"Three months, and she's washing baby clothes?" I looked at Ruby, and we both smiled.

She is driving me crazy! We had everything a baby ever needed, now was the time to set our wedding date and she was delaying. "Why don't you want to set a date?" I finally asked her.

"Because we don't know each other enough to set a date. We'll get married if you can live with me for a year and you still want to marry me."

"Amber, do you not want to marry me? Is this what all of this is about? You want to live with me but not marry me?"

"No, I do want to marry you. I love you, and I will until I take my last breath. I don't want you to feel like you have to marry me because we're having a baby."

"You know I love you. I'm happy we are having a baby because I'm having my baby with the woman I love. I wanted to marry you before I knew you were pregnant, so how about we set the date?"

"We'll set the date when you return from your mission."

"Okay, I won't be gone long, Ruby is going to stay with you while I'm away."

"Why is Ruby staying here?"

"In case you need someone, she will be here for you. I need someone to be with you or I'll worry the entire time I'm gone."

"Okay, I might do a few things to the house while you're gone, I don't particularly like having nothing to do. Maybe I'll work for Ruby and Samuel."

"No, you will not work for Ruby, that's too dangerous. I'm surprised you don't work with Jade. She has more clients than she knows what to do with them."

"Yoga, you want me to help teach yoga?"

"You do it every morning, you could teach other expecting mothers. Maybe get a spot in Jade's building."

"That's an idea, I'll run it by her."

"Yeah, ask her tonight when we are there for dinner." *Is that a secret smile on her face? It must be my imagination.* "Do we want to walk or drive?"

"Let's walk, it's so lovely outside."

"Here is your sweater, sweetheart. It'll be cool when we walk back."

"Thank you." *She still has that smile on her face.*

"Why are you smiling so?"

"I'm happy, that's why." *She's up to something.*

"Oh, there you two are, dinner will be ready in ten minutes," Opal said, meeting us on the walk over there. She put her arm through Amber's on the walk back. I wondered why Opal didn't have a boyfriend, she was beautiful. She reminded me of a woman who wasn't afraid to have curvy curves. She wore clothes that were tight and showed off her curves. She, Amber, and Jade could be triplets, they look so much alike. Jade and Ruby went out on dates, but I've never seen Opal date anyone. I'll ask Amber about it one day. I have many friends who have asked if they could date one of Amber's sisters.

"What are we having for dinner?" Amber asked Opal.

"We are having goulash with homemade buns and they smell so good right now." Opal looked at me, "Do you like goulash, Jax?

"I love it. Every time we visited my grandma, she would make it for us because she knew it was my favorite."

"Aww, I wish I could have met your grandparents," Amber said, squeezing my arm.

"You can meet them whenever you want to, they live in Miami, Florida."

"What! Your grandparents are alive?"

"Yes, they're alive."

"You never mentioned them."

"That's because when we are alone together, I only have my mind on one thing, sweetheart."

"Shhh, you'll embarrass Opal."

Opal laughed. "That doesn't embarrass me, I'm happy you have Jax."

"I wasn't referring to that, I just mean I always have you on my mind." Amber stopped walking, put her arms around me and laid her head against my chest.

"I love you so much, we'll get married when you get back from your mission." I bent my head and kissed her. When I raised my head, Opal was wiping tears off her cheeks.

"Okay, when I get home, we are getting married. Opal, you heard her and she can't take it back." We walked into the house and Opal was right, that fresh-baked bread smelled delicious. We were all sitting at the table enjoying our dinner when Amber looked at Jade.

"Jax thought I should teach expecting mothers yoga. He thought maybe I could have a spot in your building."

Every person at the table burst into laughter. I looked around and they were wiping their eyes, they laughed so damn hard. "Okay, spill the beans, what is so funny about Amber teaching yoga?"

"Are you serious? Look at Amber, she has no patience to teach anyone anything. Amber has to have a job with action," Samuel explained.

"She can train herself to have patience. She is having a baby and I can see she's getting cabin fever. We have enough baby clothes to last ten babies an entire year each. We cannot buy another piece of baby furniture, there is no room in the nursery. Give her a try."

"Okay, when do you leave on your next trip?"

"Tomorrow."

"Okay, Amber can come with me the day after tomorrow, isn't that right, Amber?"

"Yes, that's right."

"Good, now I won't have to worry. She'll have Ruby at night and Jade in the day. Thank you, you don't know what a relief it is knowing Amber will be at the yoga studio during the day."

19

AMBER

"**G**randpa, I can't sit around doing nothing, it's driving me crazy."

"You are driving me crazy. This house is sparkling. I know that my housekeepers love having you come to see me every day but it's driving me batty. Go back to work, you can do office work until you're ready to return full time. Now, go talk to your boss so you can get back to work immediately."

"You're right, thank you. I'm going to work and the chief better not say anything." *Yes, finally, someone knew what I needed.* "Thank you, Grandpa." He was chuckling as I went out the kitchen door.

GEORGE, the head of my department met me at the door of his office. "I wondered when you would be back. I knew you weren't going to quit your job. I tore your resignation up."

"Good. What can I do that isn't dull until after the baby comes?"

"You came just in time. I have a backlog of cold case files. With all this DNA evidence coming out, we need to investigate every case. Jeff and Robert got that other man Gary that got away from you that night, he confessed to killing the Jacob woman."

"That's wonderful, I'm so happy they were caught. So where are these cold files?"

"They are in the basement; I'll show you the way. You will be the only one who goes inside. You are the only one with a key, no one is allowed in there unless I tell you it's okay. It's cold down there, so be sure to bring a sweater or jacket when you come to work tomorrow."

"Dang, I didn't know we had a basement this far down. How many cases do you have?"

"Thousands, we have already captured hundreds of people who killed people. There was a man in prison since he was nineteen, he was innocent."

"How long was he in prison?"

"Thirty years."

"Thirty years, fuck! Didn't anyone believe him?"

"He had no money for a lawyer and the public defender didn't give a damn. It was a tear-jerker, let me tell you. That's when Joyce quit. It got too emotional for her. She is the one who found the real killer last year, don't you remember?"

"Yes! It was the little girl's uncle. Oh my God. But you said Joyce just quit?"

"She quit because I would have had to let her go otherwise. She was a nervous wreck. She didn't even want to go home. I want your promise that you won't become that way. Because you have a baby who needs his sleep, you also need your rest. Joyce's husband left her over her not going home."

"That's so sad."

"It was sad. Never take a file home. I will give you the

cases I want you to work on and when you finish, I will provide you with another file. Do not discuss these cases with anyone."

"I won't." *There is no way I am saying I promise because I tell my sisters everything. Besides, they might have some clues for me.* "How far down is the basement?"

"We're here." He took out three keys, there were three locks. He opened them and we walked into a cold room that was floor to ceiling nothing but files. My hand ran over all of them as I walked around the room. It went in a circle with doors, when I pulled one out, it was eight-foot long. The files were crammed inside. I saw pictures of children, and when I pulled another one, there was file after file of dead women, it never stopped.

"How do you know which ones to pick?"

"We pick the ones we need to get off the streets first. There are some sick bastards, as you know. When you get here in the morning, I will give you the keys, when you finish for the day, you bring them back to me and I'll put them in the safe. These files cover the entire state of Maine."

"Do people want in this room so bad they will break into here?"

"We've had shootouts in the hallways here, people know that DNA is catching many people who have gotten away with murder. The guilty ones come here hunting for their file. Don't tell just anyone where you work."

"I'll remember that."

"Okay, Amber, I'll see you at seven."

"Yep, I'll see you then."

Later that day, I was at Grandpa's for dinner, I wanted to spill my guts about the job I was doing but I decided not to tell them. "I've gone back to work, I'm going to be doing office work and then when I return to work after my maternity leave, I'll go back to my regular detective work."

Samuel smiled, "I knew you couldn't stay away from work that long. When do you start?" "Tomorrow morning at seven. I'm kind of excited to start."

"What will you be doing?" Ruby asked. Leave it to Ruby to ask. I didn't say anything, and her eyes got big. "Are you going to be doing something they told you not to tell anyone?"

"You're so dramatic," I said, still not answering. I was biting my tongue to keep quiet.

Jade looked at me, "What will you be doing?"

"I'm not supposed to tell anyone, but I will be working on cold cases. There are thousands."

"How come you can't tell anyone?" Axel asked.

"Because George told me not to; so please don't tell anyone else."

"Okay, I won't."

"Isn't that like in the basement?"

"Yes, I might get claustrophobic, there are no windows there."

"So, where do you start looking at something like that?"

"George will give me the cases to work on. He said it's so hard to solve a case but sometimes they get lucky. I hope I can solve a couple while I'm there."

"I'm sure you will do that department justice," Samuel said as he got up and kissed my forehead. "Tomorrow Jane is coming to dinner, can all of you be here?"

"Yes, we finally get to meet her, I can't wait," Opal said, clapping her hands. We had only met one of Samuel's lady friends since he's had us, her name was Cynthia. She took one look at us girls and wanted Samuel to give us to the foster system. Samuel took her home, and that was the end of Cynthia. I'm glad he wants us to meet Jane.

"Tell us about her?" I said, smiling at him. She has three kids, two are in college and the other one lives in Oregon. She had another child but the girl went missing at six and they never found her."

"That's horrible."

"Yes, she and her husband divorced a year later, neither of them could get over it."

"That's so sad," I said, shaking my head. "Where did they live?"

"They lived about thirty miles from here. She said three kids disappeared that year and the following year three more disappeared. It was before we moved here. Dad, do you remember when it happened?"

"Yes, I remember everything about it. After you went missing, Mama and I read everything we could about missing children. It went on for about three years. Every year, three kids would go missing, then it stopped. It didn't happen here in our town; it was a few towns over. Parents were scared to death to let their children out of their sight. It was a horrible time. It stopped about fifteen years ago."

"The girl was the oldest child."

"So, she would be twenty-three right now." I wondered if I could look up the files on those children. I better leave it alone but Samuel was stolen and now he's home again. *Get it out of your head Amber, right now. You will only do what George tells you to do. You are not going to be snooping around for children who have been missing for years.* I looked around at my sisters, and they had that look on their faces that I didn't like. I looked down so I would lose eye contact with them. I knew the minute Ruby and I started for home, Opal and Jade would follow us.

We hadn't even gotten off the porch before they joined us. "We are going to walk with you."

"Why am I not surprised?"

Opal looked at me and I knew there would be no getting out of this. She was the oldest sister and we have always followed what she wanted. "This is like fate, what if those kids are still living? Imagine if we could find them, how happy their families would be. Let's do this together, the four of us."

"Opal, you are the district attorney, you can't get mixed up in something that you could lose your job over."

"Sure I can. I don't care if I lose my job, I'm pretty tired of it anyway. I've been thinking of changing professions."

"Since when?" We all stopped to look at her.

"A few months now, but we were talking about this cold case file. You have to find those files and bring them home."

"Do you want me to get fired? This is a bad idea. Ruby, say something."

"I agree with Opal, I feel that we can solve this case. It's like we were handed this assignment from above."

"Oh, please don't even go there. Jade, say something. You know how much trouble I could get into over this. I could give birth to my child in prison, for Christ's sake."

"Oh, hush, you won't have your baby in prison. Can you sneak me in there? I could help you look for those files."

"Jade, I thought for sure you would be on my side."

"We don't have sides, we are sisters. Everything we do, we do together."

"When did you make that up?"

Jade grinned and shrugged her shoulders. "Just now."

By the time we got to Jax's home, the matter was settled. "I'll check everything out tomorrow then I'll let you know whether or not I can get into those files. We won't talk about any of this around anyone else not even Samuel or Grandpa." They all agreed and Opal and Jade walked back home. "You know Ruby, just because Jax asked you to stay with me doesn't mean you have to?"

"I know, but I like being here with you."

"Then thank you, I'm glad you are here."

20

JAX

"Kash, when you get back, can you please call Amber and tell her I'll be here longer than I thought."

"Yep, I'll check in on her for you."

"Thank you, can you give her this letter for me?" He smiled and tucked the letter into his jacket pocket.

I watched the plane take off from the hidden airstrip. Three weeks—I didn't think it would be this long, and now I don't know how much longer I'll be here. I wished I was on that plane and leaving this hot desert but we had a job to do. I looked at Angel, Trey, and Matt,

"Well, which way do we go?" I asked, climbing into the driver's seat of the jeep.

"Are you worried about Amber?" Angel asked in return.

"No, she has her sister Ruby staying with her and her family lives close by. She isn't doing detective work right now, and I have to say I'm happy she gave that up. I'm hoping she will work with Jade and teach yoga." Angel looked at me like I was crazy.

"I will bet you one thousand dollars that Amber is back at work in her department."

"What, why do you think so?"

"Because she is a homicide detective, she can't stay in one place long enough to teach yoga or anything. She'll want to kick their ass if they don't learn it as soon as she says."

Now I was worried. Her whole family thought I was silly to think that she would teach yoga and here Angel was, someone who didn't even know her well, telling me the same thing. Why didn't I just accept how she was? "Damn it, you're right," I confessed. "She probably has her gun strapped to her and is back on her job."

"Well, she did kick your butt when you tried helping her."

"Yeah, and that was the best thing that has ever happened to me. Where are we headed?"

"Keep driving until we see a sign someone put at the side of the road that says turn here."

"Are you kidding me?"

"The man I talked to said he put a sign up that says turn here. So that's all I know."

"I guess we drive until we see a sign." *Fuck, I would give anything to talk to Amber and see what she's doing. I miss her so much. I want to be there when she starts to show our baby growing inside of her. I want to see what the hell she's doing. Damn it, I want to go home.* We drove for another hour before seeing the homemade sign that said turn here. I'm surprised Matt could see it. The sun had gone down and I had to turn the lights on. We didn't like turning our headlights on because we didn't want to be noticed.

The Taliban didn't like Americans coming over to rescue anyone, Americans or Afghanistan people who helped the

Americans while in this country. We didn't find any more signs. "We will be walking if we don't find them soon," I said, looking at Matt. He was the only one awake.

"Damn, it would help if we knew what we were looking for," Matt muttered. "Maybe we should pull over until daybreak."

"Let's look for some cover where we can hide so we're not in the open," I said with my eyes darting everywhere. I saw something down a side road, so I checked it out. It looked like it was a large metal building. I pulled around the back and parked. "Let's get some sleep."

The noise woke us up. I jerked up and looked around, there were people everywhere and they were looking at us. The sun hadn't even come up yet but the lights were bright from the outside lights, on the building.

"You American?" a woman asked. She was standing about ten feet from the vehicle.

"Yes, do you know where the house of Abdul Akhtar is? We were told it's this way."

"Yes, it's here. We have come here to go to America."

"How many are here."

"It was only seven, but word got out about someone taking people to America, now everyone is coming."

I looked around at the guys, "This is not good, what are we going to do?"

"Let's find Abdul and talk to him," Trey suggested. Trey didn't like plans getting messed up. He said sloppiness caused deaths, and we agreed with him. If we had to abort this mission, we would. We went inside the building and looked around. Children were sleeping on the floor. Most of them were girls. A man came walking towards us.

"I'm so sorry, I don't know what happened. Someone told someone else, and I couldn't believe how it got out of control. People have been coming all night long. What are we going to do?"

I was so angry. I stood there trying to think. Now people were rushing inside, not even considering the sleeping children. "Stop!" I shouted. "There are sleeping children here." I looked at Abdul, "Who are the ones going with us?"

"They are in that room over there."

"The plane will not hold this many people, I need to speak with the pilot and see what he says. We'll take the ones we came here for. I'm sorry, who do all of these children belong to?"

"A bus came and dropped them off. They have the addresses of their family in America."

"I looked at Trey, we'll take as many as we can." I turned and looked back at Abdul, "Is the bus still here?"

"Yes."

"Then we'll take the kids on the bus, get them up and let me have their family information. We don't have time to argue with all these people, so load them up and we'll get going."

"Jax, we can't take these children," Matt said, shaking his head.

"Sure we can. They don't weigh as much as we do. So we'll drop them off and wait for when Kash comes back again."

"When will that be? We might be here another month."

"Angel can go back and make sure the kids are with their relatives, that way, we know they are actually related. These little girls have to marry older men. Fucking perverted bastards! Their parents knew what would happen to them. They chose to give them a chance in life. I'll follow in the jeep."

Angel didn't look too happy. "We'll let Matt go with them, Lara can help him get hold of the family members."

"That's a better idea." What the hell was I doing, I needed to be home with Amber. What if she had gone back to being a homicide detective? I looked at Matt, "Find out what Amber is doing, tell her not to do anything she isn't supposed to be doing."

"Are you fucking kidding me? I'm not telling her that. I'm sure she is working in the police headquarters taking messages."

I knew she wouldn't be taking messages; she was too curious to just sit still for too long. "Okay, okay. Can you let her know I will call her as soon as possible?"

"Yes, I'll tell her that. I will also see what she's doing and where she's working. Don't worry, we will keep an eye on her."

"Thank you, buddy, I know I can count on you."

21

AMBER

I was busy hunting through the files when I heard the door open—who could it be? I checked my gun and walked behind the wall. I watched as a woman with a black hood come around where I was. I stepped out and confronted her. She jumped and screamed, "What are you doing in here?"

"Please don't say anything, I stole one of the keys from when I worked here before. They made me quit because George said I was too involved in the case. I was involved because my sister was stolen when she was six. George didn't know Elana was my sister, then he found out and they made me leave. I did it wrong, I should have looked for her on the side but I was so emotionally involved I was staying here too long and he became suspicious," she hastened to say in a whisper.

"Is Elana one of the missing children from years back?"

"Yes, she was in the last group of kids taken. I became a police officer so I could work in this department, then I blew it. I have to have those files."

"Look, I'm not going to fight you because I'm pregnant I

will ask you to leave, but tonight I'll call you. Can you do that for me?"

"Yes, I can."

"Write your number down." When the door opened, she placed her number in my hand.

George walked in, "Nora, what are you doing here? Amber, I told you no one was allowed in here."

"When she knocked, I thought it was you. Nora told me she forgot some things here from when she worked here. She lost a bracelet that belonged to her sister, I had already handed them over to lost and found." I looked at Nora, "Be sure you check lost and found as I said."

"I will, thank you. I hope your emotions don't get the best of you as mine did."

"I am pregnant but I am a homicide detective, I see horrible things. I think it's something you never get used to seeing, I hope you find your things."

"Goodbye."

After she left, I looked at George, "Did you need to tell me something?"

"No, I saw Nora getting on the elevator and followed her."

"Why do you think she got so involved with these cases she worked on?"

"I know why she did. Her sister was taken when she was a child. The parents were working and Nora was watching her sister, they were playing in the front yard when a man walked up and took Elana. I guess Nora has always blamed herself."

"Why didn't you let her go through the files?"

"Do you know how many people have gone through those files? Every year someone wants to try and solve the kidnappings."

"How many were there?"

"Nine kids in total, three a year for three years. Then it stopped. I thought the bastard must have died; I hope he did."

"But what if he's alive and can tell you where those kids are?"

"I don't believe he is, I tried for years to find that bastard. I couldn't even get a hint of a clue. Even though Nora was there and saw the back of the man, she didn't see his face. He wore a dark hood and threw the screaming little girl into the back seat and the car left. Someone had to be the driver. The only thing we have is the vehicle was white, that's it. The others were taken when no one was around. Nora is the only one who has seen anything. Her neighbor ran after her as she ran down the street screaming that a man had taken her sister."

"That must have been a nightmare for her, how old was she?"

"She was ten. We all know how fucked up life can get. Look at your life. Look at Samuel's life. He was taken and he didn't realize where his dad was for years. He was lucky, most children missing all these years are not as fortunate as Samuel."

"What a sad story. Do you think it was the same person who took Samuel?"

"No, the man who took Samuel was a child molester. He took him for one reason, hisown pleasure. Samuel did the right thing by running away. The man would have killed him and gotten a younger child."

I thought back to that night when I was little, and I over-heard Liam and Samuel talking one night. Liam went and killed that man that hurt Samuel. I had forgotten once in a while it would pop my in my head. I remembered it when I was in the hospital, but decided not to mention it to anyone. I think that is why Samuel took care of us at first. Then he loved us as much as we loved him. I would never breathe a word of what I heard that night. I didn't know how he hurt Samuel at the time but as I grew older, I understood, and I was glad Liam killed him.

"I'll let you get back to work," George interrupted my thoughts. How is it going for you? I know it's only been three weeks, but what do you think about this job?"

"As soon as my baby is born and I can go back to work, I'll take my old job any day." George was still laughing as he went out the door. As soon as the door shut, I called Nora.

"Hello."

"Nora, this is Amber, can you tell me where those files are?"

"Yes, they are under nine missing children, all in one file. I put them together before I left. Go to the back of the room, you'll have to get the step stool, I put them behind the files of abused children."

"Okay, I'll take a look at them." I would never have found this file without Nora's help. I opened the file and copied everything to my phone. I had a good feeling about this, like what I was doing would work out the way we wanted it to.

I went back to the file George gave me. This was a woman who was brutely murdered eight years ago. The poor woman was beaten so severely that her face was unrecognizable. They had to use fingerprints to ID her. I poured over the papers when I realized I saw another one of these cases. Two years ago, when I was working on another case where the woman was in the same position and beaten so severely, her sister recognized her hand with her rings. They got fingerprints and knew who she was. *Is this the same person who killed both women?* I called George to come down to the basement.

"George, take a look at this file. Do you remember when we found that woman a couple of years ago? She had the same injuries as this woman. Are there any more files like this one?"

George walked around the room until he found the files he was looking for. If there were more like this, we would have a serial killer running loose. I watched as George pulled out two more files, one was five years ago, the other seven years ago and the murder I worked on two years ago. That made four women killed the same way, left in the same position, naked with their hands and feet tied with baling wire.

I looked at George as we went through these files together. "I think whoever we are looking for must have something to do with farming, it's convenient for him to carry baling wire."

"Yep, I agree. Do these women have anything in common?"

I shrugged my shoulders. "I don't know, but you better believe I'm going to find out. Am I allowed to question the families?"

"Yes, as long as you aren't in any danger. Your friends keep calling me to make sure you're not doing anything dangerous."

"I know, isn't that sweet, I'm sure Jax must have talked them into it. I have them stopping at my house every night to make sure I'm in for the night. As soon as Jax gets home, there will be a wedding. I'll let you know the date; I want you and Brenda at my wedding."

"Thank you, we wouldn't miss it. I'll leave you to solve this case, I have to head out on a homicide across town.

What has become of our town? There have already been three murders this year."

I took photos of what I would need to talk to the families of the murdered women. Then I took down the missing children's files, I was reading through each one when my phone rang giving me a huge fright. I jumped and dropped it before I answered. "Hello."

"Amber, how soon can you come and check this murder out? I think we have another victim."

"I'll be there as soon as I can." I wrote the address down and put away all those files. Then I walked out to my car and drove to where George was. As I pulled up, I saw Jeff. He spotted me and shook his head.

"What the hell are you doing here? I told Jax I would keep you away from crime scenes."

"George called me. This murder might tie in with a cold case file I'm working on."

"Oh yeah, do you want to tell me about it?"

"You know I can't discuss anything I read in the dungeon. Why do they have to keep those files there? And why is it always cold there?"

"Are you trying to change the subject?"

"Yes, now, show me where the victim is."

"Follow me. I have to tell you, this is gruesome, so prepare yourself."

I knew it would be horrible but looking at the photos and the real thing isn't anywhere close to what I saw just then. I felt my stomach roll as I looked at the woman lying on the ground, tied with baling wire. She was positioned in the same way as the others, her face smashed in. I looked at George, "You should call the FBI, we have a serial killer on our hands."

"Damn, I knew you would say that. We'll hand this case over to them."

"Okay, I think I will get back to the office."

This case would haunt me forever. I turned around and started taking photos of the poor woman who became the victim of a crazy man. Then I started looking for anything to do with a farmer. I saw a piece of what looked like hay, and when I looked at the woman's blood-soaked hair, I saw more wheat or hay.

"I thought you were leaving," George said three times before I realized he was talking to me.

"Come over here. See that piece of hay? And there in her hair is more. She must have been in the back of his truck. You know how farmers carry hay bales in the back of their vehicles? This is an angry farmer, probably jilted by a fiancée or his wife left him. Or he killed her. The urge to murder someone becomes uncontrollable after a few years, so he gives in to the pressure and kills another woman he believes deserves it."

"You're outstanding," Jeff said, looking at me with a grin. "So, are we working together again?"

"No, I'm pregnant. I have to put my baby first but this will not stop me from solving these murders. Don't let anyone else around this area, I believe there will be more clues. He might have met these women on an online dating app, I'll talk to her family and see what they say."

George chuckled, "It doesn't matter what job I give you; it will always have an element of danger because you dig deep until you find the killer."

"I hope I find the killer. I'm going to go through those files with a fine-tooth comb, as the old saying goes. We'll catch this bastard." *And the other ones with the missing children.*

"I'll see you back at the office. Have you given any more thought to talking to those women's family members?"

"Yes, I'm going to call them and see if I can ask them a few questions."

"Okay, let me know what you find."

"I will. Goodbye Jeff. Please take photos of her fingers and toes. Check to see if she had just shaved her legs. Do a rape test, it might not have been rape, but it will show if they had sex. And if they did, and he is in the database, we will have his DNA." I walked back to my vehicle deep in thought, I didn't notice Matt until I was at my truck.

"Hello Amber, are you back working detective work?"

"No, I work in the office, but George wanted me to see this woman. Have you heard anything from Jax?"

"No, Kash will be going back tomorrow, hopefully this time he can bring all of them home."

"I hope so, I miss him so much."

"What part of the office work are you doing?"

I looked at Matt, debating whether or not to tell him, then I made a decision. I pulled him back over to his truck, "I'm working on cold case files. I'm not supposed to tell anyone, but I know I can trust you. I was working on an unsolved murder case when I realized I saw the same kind of murder two years ago and then we found two more files with the same thing. And then today it's the same as the others. We have a serial killer."

"Do not get involved in this case, it might get you and the baby killed. Serial killers go after anyone trying to solve the murder. Hell, he could be watching you standing here talking to me. Stay out of this. The cold case files are a deadly place to work, I'm surprised George gave you this job."

"He did tell me not to tell anyone."

"But you told me."

"Because I trust you."

"Who else do you trust?"

"My family."

"Damn it, Amber, you need to stop right now. There are others out there to solve this case." I walked around and got inside his vehicle.

"Let's get a hamburger, and I'll fill you in." I heard him chuckle as he backed out and turned towards the in-and-out burger. "These are my favorite hamburgers."

"Mine too, now tell me what is going on?"

"I noticed all the murdered women were tied up with baling wire, so naturally, it belonged to a farmer. Who else would have a surplus of baling wire that is conveniently around them? Then today, the murdered woman has hay in her hair. Like she was in the back of a truck. I think I can solve this in a couple of weeks."

"Holy hell, this is worse than Jax thought. What you are doing, you might as well wear a sign that says, 'Serial killer come and get me, I'm going to catch you!'"

I chuckled. All these Rangers were the same. He pulled into the drive-through window and I ordered us a burger with fries and a large Pepsi. We ate in the vehicle and Matt kept looking at me like he wanted to ask me something. "What?"

"I probably don't want to know the answer to this question, but are you working on any other cases?"

"Not any that I'm supposed to be working on but yes, we are."

"We?"

"My sisters and I, and maybe Nora, too. I'm still debating on that one."

"Who is Nora?"

"Nora used to work on the cold case files. She worked her way into the job because her sister was stolen when she was five. I think Nora was ten. She was babysitting." He held up his hand.

"I don't want to know anymore, I'm familiar with this case. A friend of mine had his sister taken from the last group of kids."

"That's when Nora's sister was taken."

"It would be best if you stopped digging in those cases. If whoever got a whiff of you and your sisters opening up his cold case, he might come after all of you."

"Thank you for thinking about our welfare, but we won't let anyone know."

"You told me."

"Because I trust you," I saw him shaking his head.

We drove back to my vehicle, and Matt looked at me. "Listen to me, I think you would do better if you taught yoga with your sister."

"That's all undercover, don't tell anyone, but Jade and Ruby are private investigators. The yoga place is a front, it's what they want people to think is their business. Opal is going to go in with them. She gave notice at her job. I might also work with them. But first, I need to talk with Jax about it."

"You be careful."

"I will be. Thank you for lunch."

"You're welcome."

22

JAX

I paced back and forth in the small room. I knew I had made a path on the floor, but when Kash returned and told me everything Matt said about Amber's job, I couldn't relax. Surely, she knew how dangerous it was trying to solve a cold case. Those people didn't want that case reopened and they would do anything to keep it closed. She had the serial killer and the people who stole those kids. I needed to get home and protect her, for crying out loud!

First, we had to get out of here. It'd been six days since Kash got here, and it was too dangerous for us to leave. Someone tipped the Taliban off we were here, and they were searching everywhere for us. The plane was confiscated, so we were stuck here until someone came for us unless we found another plane. I looked at Kash. "How did she get involved with finding the persons who took the kids? That was years ago."

I saw Trey roll his eyes and knew I didn't blame him. I heard the answer to that question four times since Kash showed up here.

"I'll tell him this time," Trey said, rolling his shoulders. "Samuel's new girlfriend had her child stolen when she was six. The crazy sisters thought when Amber got the job working in the cold case files it was fate. And if that wasn't enough to make them believe fate played a role in everything, the woman who got fired had a sister who was stolen. So they were going to find the kidnappers of those nine children. But wait, I'm not finished; since she worked in that department, she discovered the similarities to other murders. Then a couple of weeks ago, another woman was murdered, which made her realize it was a serial killer. Amber is determined to solve these cold cases," he held up his hand, "don't forget she did tell Matt she would be careful because she would never let any harm come to her child."

I chuckled. When Amber was determined to do something, she did it. "God, I love that woman."

Kash laughed. "Yeah, don't forget how she tricked Matt into buying her lunch. She climbed in his truck and told him she needed a hamburger and the in-and-out burger was her favorite place to eat hamburgers."

I was going to leave this place. I looked at the others, "We need to get out of here. We can't stay in this room forever or they will find us. Too many people know we are here. As soon as it's dark, we need to leave."

"I agree," Angel said. "I want to be with my wife and daughter. Abdul said he would be back in a couple of days, that was three days ago. Either he got caught or it's not safe for him to come back. Let's get some rest before our long hike tonight."

We all slept for a few hours and then got as much as we could pack in our backpacks. We knew we had to carry water and food. Since we only had protein bars, we packed our bags with water and headed out. We walked until the sun started to rise, and then we found some shade to rest under. We took turns keeping watch so all of us could get some sleep before night came. When the sun went down, we walked. We did this for two nights when we saw the plane. We went to where our plane used to be, now it was burned to the ground, only the metal was there. I knew it would be a place that would always be watched.

"We'll have to find a new area to fly in and out of. When do you think Matt will be here?" I asked anyone who thought they knew the answer.

"He won't be getting concerned until Hunter doesn't get his call. Then they'll come looking for us. We need to get a phone that we can use to call out."

"Let's try ours, even if they track them, we will be able to let the others know where we are." I took out my phone and dialed Matt.

"Where the hell are you?" he asked when he picked up.

"They found out about us. Don't come to the same spot. They burned our plane down. Where are you now?"

"Germany. Go to that tiny airstrip where we picked up Lara."

"We're on foot, and we travel at night, so give us at least three days." We confirmed everything then I hung up.

We looked around and started walking, hoping the airstrip was still there. We saw dust in the distance and took cover in some underbrush. We stayed there for four hours before we decided to leave.

The sun was down, but we moved quietly in case they were watching the area. We moved slower than we wanted, but we had no choice. It had to be dark, with no twilight. I looked at the compass and pointed to the left. On the fourth night, we spotted the small plane hidden behind trees, we knocked on the door and Conner opened it.

"We need to get out of here, they are out there hunting us." We jumped inside and the plane coasted out onto the runway. That's when we saw headlights coming toward us. "Go! I shouted, "let's get out of here before it's too late. They'll start shooting, so stay low." No sooner was that out of my mouth than the bullets started flying. I saw Kash jerk and knew he was hit. I pulled him out of the driver's seat and jumped in his place. I knew we would have to land once we got out of this country. Trey sat in the co-pilot's seat and started pushing buttons. The instrument panel was all over the place. I wasn't sure what was hit. I just knew it wasn't good.

"Can you land this without the wheels coming down?"

"I can, as soon as we are out of this country. I don't think they hit the fuel tank, so we should be fine. How is Kash?"

"He'll be fine, he got hit in the shoulder."

"What happened to that rescue you were leaving on? I'm going as soon as we get home. I was supposed to be there a couple of days ago. So whoever I was supposed to meet up with is probably angry. Hopefully, they are still in hiding."

"Where are you going?"

"Sudan, there are a bunch of kids that need help getting out of the country. I believe they are getting help from a teacher or mentor or someone I'm not sure who he is. I can only hope he doesn't slow me down when the time comes that we have to run."

"I wish you success and speed. I, for one, can't wait to see Amber. I hope she hasn't got herself mixed up in something dangerous. Hell, it's been almost two months since I was home. No telling what she's up to without me to keep her safe."

"I'm sure she's fine. If I remember right, all four of the sisters can kick ass. By the way, I'm not sure if I'll make it to the wedding but congratulations."

"Thank you."

23

AMBER

"Ruby, you cannot check on anything until I get home. I wish I never showed you any of those files. I'm on my way home, for Pete's sake! Please don't leave until I get there." *I swear I am so mad at myself for letting my sisters talk me into helping me out.* I had just turned down the road to our home when my phone rang. I pushed the button on my steering column, thinking it was another one of my sisters.

"No, you have to wait until I get home."

I heard a chuckle and I let out a sob. I pulled off the road and cried. "Sweetheart, I'm on my way home. I'll be there in a few days, please don't cry. Why are you crying?"

I sniffed and wiped my nose with my sleeve. "Jax, my sisters are driving me crazy. I have a new job working on cold cases. Well, I let my sisters talk me into helping me find who took the nine kids. This happened years ago. I copied the files of these children—I knew I wasn't supposed to copy any files but I did it because we wanted to find those missing children and now I wish I hadn't. Anyway, let's not talk about all that. You don't know what it means to be hearing your voice right now. When are you coming home? The baby is growing and I miss you so much. I love you. I need you to talk to my sisters and straighten them out." I sniffed and wiped my nose and my tears.

"Take a breath, sweetheart. Don't upset the baby, I'll take care of everything. I love you too. I want you to take some time off work."

"I can't, I'm so close to catching a serial killer."

"Amber, please get off that case right now. He will come after you if he knows you are close to catching him."

"I'll be careful, I promise. I already told Matt I would be careful."

"Can you please wait until I get home?"

"Jax, you know that would give the killer a chance to kill someone else. It will be best if you didn't worry about me. I'm a homicide detective, I know what I'm doing. Besides, my sisters are helping me with that case also."

"Dear lord, sweetheart, I will call your sisters right now. Please don't do anything before I get home. I'll help you. I need to go sweetheart. We are boarding the plane, I love you."

"I love you too. I'll see you when you get here." My phone was beeping again, so I answered the phone.

"Where are you?" Ruby demanded. "I have to get ready for my date."

"Jax called me, so I pulled over to talk to him. I'll be there in two minutes."

"Oh, Jax is on the phone with Opal, I think he's making her angry. Her face is turning red. She hung up on him. Oh lord, she's angry."

I pulled into grandpa's driveway and wiped my tears. Opal stormed down the steps to my door. I opened it and looked at her. She looked like she was going to cry. "What happened?"

"He yelled at me. He said if we didn't stop this foolishness, you and the baby could get hurt. I'm sorry, he's right. What is the matter with me? I was so excited I didn't think."

I threw my hand up. "Oh, poof, Jax is not right. He won't be home for a few days. I'm not going to wait that long. We have a date with the farmer tonight. Why don't you let me go?"

"No, I'm going," Ruby said. "If he comes after me, I'll kill him."

"Ruby, don't turn your back on him, he might put something in your drink."

"I won't take my eyes off him, plus you three will be in the room. You don't have to worry about me, I've trained since I was two how to fight. I have my gun in my bag and my taser." Ruby looked beautiful. Every time I see her dressed up the way she is right now, I think of Jane Russel. She had red lip gloss on, I knew the guy's eyes would bulge. The dress Ruby had on showed off all of her curves. I looked at Jade and Opal and smiled. They were both dressed to kill.

"I have you a dress inside, hurry, let's change."

"My dresses are tight."

"You can wear one of mine."

"Why do you think yours will fit?"

"I have a couple I wore after I had Axel, they will fit you perfectly."

I wasn't so sure about that. Opal wore dresses to show off her figure. I didn't want to draw too much attention to us. I let her talk me into wearing her dress. I had to keep pulling the bodice up, I felt like I was showing too much of my breast. Opal slapped my hand, "Leave it alone. You are looking down that's why you see so much. Looking at you from where I stand, you can't see as much."

"What if I stand next to a man?"

"That's what these shoes are for." I looked at her heels. I slipped into the shoes and felt beautiful. I did like getting dressed up. We went downstairs and Samuel whistled.

"We'll be home early, Axel. I want your homework finished before dinner."

"I will, Mom. You look beautiful."

"Thank you, sweetheart."

"You always look beautiful."

"Who needs a man when you have a son who tells you how beautiful you are."

"All of you are beautiful."

"Thank you, Axel," we said together.

We arrived at the restaurant in separate vehicles, just in case the farmer was already there waiting. We went inside first, and then Ruby came in fifteen minutes later. She asked if her date was there and she was taken to a table where an older man sat; he didn't look anything like his photo. Ruby didn't give anything away that she was surprised by his age. I knew he was the man we were looking for. I felt it, and my heart started pumping fast. People were looking at Ruby and us. We might have overdressed for this restaurant. I felt someone looking at us, so I looked around, and a good-looking man was sitting in the corner watching us. He kept looking at Ruby. I had a hunch that he was watching over us. I stood up and walked to his table.

"Has Jax got you guarding us?"

"Damn, you are good."

I wanted to stomp my foot. "You don't have to stay here. We can take care of ourselves. You can tell Jax I said so."

I'm sorry, I can't leave, I made a promise."

"Fine, but don't mess this up. That guy is a serial killer and I'm locking him up. This is my case, Jax is going to have to realize I don't take orders. What's your name?"

"Asher Wright."

"Are you a Ranger?"

"Yes."

"Then I have to be nice because you are Jax's friend." He nodded, but he didn't take his eyes off of Ruby. I walked back to the table and saw him looking at his phone.

"Who's that?"

"Asher Wright, he's Jax's friend. We'll ignore him."

"How are we going to do that? He's coming straight towards us."

I looked over, and he sat down at our table. "I decided to take you up on your offer to share your table."

"I did not offer to share our table."

"I know, but when I sent Jax a photo of you ladies, he told me to get over here and wrap my jacket around you to hide your chest from all these male eyes."

I spit wine on the table. I looked at Opal, "I told you this dress was too low. Now Jax has brought attention to my breast." The hot guy chuckled.

"Oh, for Pete's sake! You said we were going to ignore what Jax said, introduce us to your friend."

"He isn't my friend. I guess he kind of is my friend since he's Jax's friend. Asher Wright, these are my sisters Opal and Jade Martin. That one sitting over there is Ruby, she is the youngest of us, she is also the most stubborn. Or she wouldn't be sitting there; I would be. She thought if I were there, he would recognize us as being related. I guess that makes sense, we look alike."

"So why do you believe he's the killer?"

"We put a few clues together. This isn't the first farmer

we've met up with, but I just have a feeling that he is our killer. I have a feel for these things," I whispered. "My heart started beating fast, that's the first sign. The second sign is I looked inside his vehicle, all the women were tied up with baling wire, and there was hay in the truck. The woman we found last month had hay in her hair. That's how I knew he was a farmer."

He took his eyes off of Ruby for just a second. "Jax told me you were expecting a baby, it would be best if you were more careful. You shouldn't be hunting down serial killers; I'll take over from here."

I heard Opal chuckle. "Why do I feel like I'm talking to Jax, are you texting him?"

"No, but I know what he would say. He loves you very much," Asher said looking at Amber.

"Did he tell you that?" I was curious.

"Yes, he's told everyone who would listen."

Jade cleared her throat. "He's working you, Amber."

I saw when Ruby excused herself and went to the restroom. I followed. I didn't know Asher also followed. Opal and Jade watched Ruby's drink to see if he had put anything in it.

"Ruby, you weren't supposed to leave the table," I said as soon as we got in the bathroom. That's when I knew Asher followed us. Ruby watched him for a moment, then she looked at me.

"I couldn't help it; I have to pee. Can you wait outside while I use the restroom?" she asked Asher.

"You'll be in a stall, you won't even know I'm here."

"Are you kidding me?" I watched as Ruby looked him up and down, then she turned and walked into the stall and started singing so he couldn't hear her pee. We grinned at one another. When she came out, she washed her hands. "Who are you?"

"Asher Wright."

"But who are you?"

"He's Jax's friend."

"I should have known." She was still standing before him. Neither was moving, then he bent his head and kissed her. As I watched, Ruby put her arms inside his jacket and around him. I didn't say anything at first then I cleared my throat two times before Asher raised his head. Their eyes never left each other. Finally, Asher stepped back.

"Don't drink your drink," he told her, then he turned and walked out.

I looked at Ruby, "Why didn't you kick him back when he kissed you?"

"I don't know." She wiped a tear away. "Oh, my God, I've found him."

"What? No, he's just like Jax. You know how Jax drives you crazy."

"Yes, forget I said that. I was crazy for a minute, now I'm back to my old self."

She walked out of the restroom and I waited a moment before following her. As Ruby sat down, she knocked her glass of wine over, I looked over at Asher, he looked the same, except he had a tick moving in his jaw. I was sure he was mentally kicking his ass for that unexpected kiss.

I saw the farmer raise his hand and order Ruby another wine, when the waiter got there, Ruby told him she wanted a beer. I snickered; I couldn't help myself. I saw Asher smile. Then our food arrived. We were eating when my phone rang.

"I miss you."

"Did you wrap Asher's jacket around you?"

"No, I did not. I can't talk about him because he's eating dinner at our table."

Jax laughed. "Who has he taken a shine to, Opal or Jade?"

"Ruby. When are you coming home?"

"I'll be there in two days. Asher is staying with you until I get home."

"I'm not going to discuss it with you, hurry back. I love you."

"I love you, sweetheart."

I blinked my eyes to keep from crying. Opal started talking when she saw my eyes blinking. She knew I was close to tears.

"What did you do before joining the Rangers," she asked Asher.

"I was a homicide detective."

"Really, why did you stop being a homicide detective?" I asked.

"Does anyone ever stop? I'm always trying to solve cases, the same as you. You work in the cold case files, but here you are, back at being what you are."

"Yeah, I didn't last anytime away from the job. As soon as I walked back into the department, I knew I couldn't quit. Maybe after the baby is born, I might work with my sisters."

"What do you sisters do?" he asked Jade.

"We are private investigators."

"Oh yeah? How's business?"

"We put things on hold, we didn't want Amber doing this alone. Plus, we are hunting down the man who kidnapped the kids."

I shook my head, "Jade, don't you remember that was a secret? Those files were not supposed to be seen by anyone but me. And I didn't even have permission to look at them."

"I know, but Asher is an ex-detective, he won't tell anyone. Will you?" she asked, looking at him.

"Let me get this straight, you are working in the cold case files, and you four are trying to solve the cases? Is it just a couple, or will you try solving all of them?"

"Yes."

"Yes, just as couple or yes, all of them?"

"Jade, do not say another word. Of course, we aren't trying to solve all of them, it's only two cases."

"Does the head of your department know what you are doing?"

"Not really, he gave me a case of the first murdered victim of the farmer, I discovered a few more of them and we decided to bring him out into the open and catch him."

"You four are playing a dangerous game. Why don't you tell whoever is in charge and let them take over?"

"I am in charge," I said. "Just because I'm pregnant doesn't mean I don't know what I am doing."

"I'm not saying that you don't know what you are doing, I just think you should be more careful."

I saw Ruby stand up and I knew her dinner date was over. I saw movement in my periphery and realized Asher also stood up. He took Jade's hand and pulled her to her feet and they followed Ruby outside. I could see them through the window. He talked to Jade, standing by a vehicle I thought must be his. It was a huge truck. The Rangers all loved trucks, probably because they were big enough for them to fit inside comfortably.

I saw Ruby get into her car and drive away. Asher and Jade followed her and we followed the farmer. He followed behind the other two vehicles. Opal got on her phone and called Jade. "Hey, you should turn down a different street, he's following behind you," I said, talking into the speaker.

I saw them turn onto another street, then they pulled over and turned off the lights. I followed behind the man following Ruby. "Do you think he's going to follow her home?"

"It looks like it," Opal said.

"Call Ruby," I said to my vehicle.

"Hello, I see him, I'm going to Jax's house. I told him I live alone. I want to see what he will do."

"Okay, we'll be right behind you." We kept driving and I saw Asher pull in behind us. "Call Opal."

"Hey, Ruby's going to Jax's house, we want to see if he follows her. She told him she lived alone..." I heard Asher swearing, he was saying something about crazy women.

"We're right behind you."

"I know, I see you. Don't get close enough that he notices we are following him."

I heard Asher talking, "Tell her I know what to do." I chuckled and hung up the phone.

When Ruby pulled into the driveway, the man turned his lights out and slowly drove past the house. I went around him so he wouldn't think I was watching him. When I was far enough, I turned around and drove back. "Call Samuel."

"Hello?"

"Samuel, the man is watching Ruby at Jax's house. I know she can handle him, but can you run over there? I have these stupid heels and this tight dress on." I looked at Opal. "This is why I don't wear these outfits; you never know when you have to run somewhere. I'm taking these damn shoes off and running back." I slipped out of my shoes and hiked the dress up. I looked over at Opal, and she did the same thing. Both of us were hanging close to the shoulder, so that if he drove by, we could hide. I heard shouting, took off running and stopped in my tracks when I got to the driveway. It was Ruby and Asher shouting at each other. The man lay on the ground, knocked out. Asher looked like he was going to have a black eye.

Jade walked over to us and shrugged her shoulders. "Ruby said she didn't know it was him running at her, and she walloped him a good one right in his eye."

"He kissed her in the restroom, but I have to say she kissed him back, she even put her arms around him."

"Amber, why are you telling them?" she moaned.

"I'm explaining why you hit him."

"I didn't know it was him."

"You can stop lying, I know you knew it was me," Asher said. He had a grin on his face.

"I called the police," Samuel said. "George is also on his way here. You two might want to pull your dress down." I heard Asher and Ruby chuckle and Opal and I looked down. Our dresses were pulled up to the top of our thighs, we both grinned. George came to a screeching halt right behind us.

"You almost hit us," I said the moment he was out of his car.

"Are you sure it's him?"

I looked at Ruby. "Yes, I taped his conversation. He blames everything on his wife who left him. He tracked her down and she was his first murdered victim." He started waking up and Asher grabbed him. He turned him around and George read him his rights. When the police pulled into the driveway, the man was screaming about Ruby trying to kill him, when he followed her home to kill her.

"I'll take the confession with me," George said, holding his hand out.

"You'll have to wait until I copy it," Ruby said.

"When will that be?" George asked.

"Let me see your phone." All of us held our phones out as Ruby played the message back. We all copied the message so it wouldn't get lost.

"Well, that's one case solved," I said, looking at George.

"That was a damn good job, detective. I'll have another one for you in the morning."

"I'll get your car," Samuel said.

I looked at Asher, "You won't have to stay tonight, the killer is locked up."

"That's not what Jax told me. He said for me to stay until he's home."

Ruby looked at Asher. "Jax said for me to stay here, so you won't need to stay."

"Sorry," he shrugged his shoulders, "I'll sleep on the sofa."

"You won't have to sleep on the sofa, there are plenty of rooms. Now I have to put my baby to bed; she's tired, I said looking at them."

"Amber, say something."

"I already did, thank you everyone for all of your help. Goodnight."

24

JAX

The house was quiet as I unlocked it and walked upstairs. I walked straight to our room where I knew Amber would be. I didn't make it to my room before someone kicked me. "Damn it, Ruby, why did you do that?"

I heard someone chuckle behind me and turned around. Asher stood there in his blue jeans and no shirt, he had a black eye.

"She probably thought you were me."

"What did you do to get that black eye?"

"He kissed her," Amber said, putting her arms around me. "Say goodnight Jax, we need some sleep." Sleep was the last thing on my mind. I kissed her right there as I pulled her into my arms. We walked to our room and left Asher and Ruby standing there.

When we finally went downstairs, they were both gone. "They didn't say goodbye," I said, looking at Amber. "Let's go back to bed."

I put my arms around her and spread my hands across her tummy. "I can feel the baby growing."

"Yes, she will be here in three more months."

"Did you find out if we are having a girl?"

"No, I just feel like she's a girl. My father will be here with Reese and Luke at the end of the month. Should we get married while they are here? I would like to have my brother be there with us. I want him to know that I love him and that he's included in all of our lives."

"I wanted to be married sooner than the end of the month but that sounds great. We will get married as soon as the rest of your family gets here. I want to go to the doctor with you when you go. I'm going to be there with you the entire time."

"I love you. Did I tell you about the case of the missing kids?"

"Yes, they would be grown-ups now if they are still living. You aren't going to work on any more of these dangerous cases. I can't believe you chased the serial killer down."

"Well, that one was almost thrown in my face. The poor woman who worked with the cold cases before me spent her entire time hunting for her sister, I don't think she did much more than that. Poor Nora: she blames herself for her sister being missing because she was babysitting at the time. She was ten, and Elana was five. Her mother worked all the time. They had no father, so they got by the best they could."

"Ten years old, she was so young."

"Yeah, she was. Imagine dealing with that at such a young age."

"Amber, you can't fix everything, you need to remember that."

"I know. I'm going to interview the families and see if there was anything in common among them."

"Does your boss know?"

"No, but I'm going to tell him today. What are you doing today?"

"I'm meeting with the guys. I won't be going anywhere. Conner is going to Sudan to rescue some kids who went there with their school. Who the fuck would allow their children to go to a war zone on a school trip? He said the teacher ran off or something and the kids were stranded there. They are hiding out in a church somewhere. He'll have to find the place; he doesn't have directions. He'll manage though."

"I hope he finds them soon."

"Yeah, me too. I hate the thought of children being in danger. But sugar, let's stop talking shop now. Let's talk about something less daunting."

"I agree. Hmm, what shall we talk about... Oh, did I tell you when Asher kissed Ruby in the bathroom?"

"In the bathroom, what bathroom?"

"He followed us to the women's bathroom at the restaurant. Ruby left her table, I excused myself and went in there. Asher walked in behind me. He kissed her, I was in shock, waiting for Ruby to let him have it, but she wrapped her arms around him inside his jacket. I had to clear my throat twice before he raised his head. It was the strangest thing. He had never even talked to her."

"I wanted to do that the first time I saw you."

"You did not."

"I would have kissed you right there in that parking lot if you hadn't been kicking me."

She gave out such a boisterous laugh, I would think she was mocking me if I didn't know better. "It's after lunch, I have to go," Amber finally said, wrapping her arms around me. "Let's both come home early."

"Okay, I'll see you in a few hours."

As soon as she left, I got in my truck and went to see Ruby. I met them all in the kitchen; they were having lunch. Samuel made me a plate and a glass of iced tea. "Ruby, what kind of business are you doing?"

"Why?"

"I'm just asking."

"Jade, Opal, and I have a private investigation business. We solve crimes, among other things. Now tell me why you have asked?"

"I don't want you to get Amber into anything that will cause her and the baby harm. I love her and I love all of you. You are all my family now, so please keep me informed of whatever you are doing so I can help you."

"We love you too, otherwise I would kick you out for telling us what we should and shouldn't do," she teased, then she hugged me. "Now, you mean that you want us to make sure we don't bring Amber into any danger."

"Isn't that what I said?"

"We were with her this time because she would have done it on her own if we hadn't gotten involved."

"She is so stubborn. All I want is for her to be safe but she's not listening to anything I say. Thank you by the way. This food is excellent. Who cooked lunch?"

"Grandpa."

"Thank you, Grandpa. I missed your cooking. Amber and I are getting married at the end of the month."

Everyone clapped and I had to stand up and get hugs from everyone. Samuel, I noticed, wiped his eyes. I looked at him. "Samuel, I want to thank you for raising these women to be who they are today. You've done a job you should be proud of. I hope I'm as good a parent as you are."

"Jax, thank you so much for that, I'm sure you will be an excellent father."

"I swear you used to irritate me but I'm starting to like you," Ruby said, smiling. Now what's going on?"

"Amber is going after whoever kidnapped those children years ago, if I'm not with her, can one of you be?"

"What kids?" Samuel said, looking at each of us.

"When she started working on the cold case files, the woman before her was taken off of the cases because she was obsessed with finding who took her sister. Now Amber is going to start interviewing all of the family members."

"Wait, are you saying she's going to try and find the kidnapper from fifteen years ago? Is it because my girlfriend has a child that was kidnapped? She was one of those missing children. I'm not sure I want you bringing all of that up again."

"Some parents still have hope that their child is alive: look at how Grandpa was when we all showed up here. The only thing he cared about was that his child was alive. If we can find who took them, maybe we can find them."

"Let them do this," Grandpa said. "My heart was dead until Samuel came back home."

"Okay, you can help Amber but tell us when you get close to the kidnapper if he's still alive. I don't want anything happening to you girls."

"Thanks for lunch, I have a meeting I need to be at, I'll see you later. I would also like to say I'm happy we live close to you."

"You keep this kind of talk up, I'm going to kiss you," Samuel said.

I laughed as I walked outside thinking how lucky I am to now be related to this family.

When I pulled into Angel's driveway, I saw Asher backing out. "Where are you off to?"

"I have a family emergency, I'll be gone for a while," he

looked like he wanted to say more, so I stood there waiting. He changed his mind because he waved his hand and drove away. It was good to be home. I would be a married man at the end of the month. I was a fortunate man, all I had to do was keep my new family from getting themselves killed. I knew I would have my hands full but I had the best woman a man could have by his side and a baby on the way.

THE END

If you enjoyed Jax, keeping reading for more of Trey.

TREY
   https://www.amazon.com/dp/B09YVVRT1J

25

TREY

That one night of hot, sweaty sex stayed on my mind constantly. I couldn't stop berating myself for not getting her name and phone number. We agreed that we would have one fabulous night without any strings attached. So I called her gorgeous, and she called me green eyes. I have never had a night like that in my life. It wasn't just the sex. I know this sounds crazy, but it was like our souls connected.

I wondered if she even thought about me. Probably not. She was so damn hot she could have any man she wanted. I wished she wouldn't have left the hotel room while I slept. She was perhaps ashamed of having sex with a stranger. I didn't usually pick up strange women and take them to a hotel, but I couldn't do anything else when I saw this woman drinking a shot of whiskey. I wanted her, and my body needed her. She felt the same strong pull between us.

"Damn, it, Trey. Are you still thinking about that woman? It's been two years already," Conner said, shaking his head.

"I can't help where my mind goes when it's idle. Besides,

I saw her at Hunter's wedding. I told you that. She had a baby, and a man stood by her side. She was more beautiful than I thought. Maybe she's married, so she didn't want us to exchange names. Whatever the reason, I was determined to find out her name. She acted like she had no idea who I was. I didn't see a ring, but I'm sure she was with him. He must have been the father to the baby. So I didn't ask Charlie who she was."

"Then forget her."

"I have already done that. I'm seeing a woman. Her name is Sandy. She owns the Sea Chest restaurant. I've been seeing her for a couple of months now. So my mind isn't always on gorgeous," Conner didn't need to know I made that little lie up.

"I'm glad to hear it. Let's go; we have a long walk ahead of us."

I forced my mind not to think of that beautiful woman I was with one night. I've had sex with more women than her. I don't understand why she stayed in my memory, and knowing she was friends with Charlie and Hunter didn't help. I wanted to ask Charlie about her, but I shut my mouth. After all, what would I say? *You know your beautiful friend, I had fantastic sex with her for one long night, and I can't stop thinking of her. Yeah, that would get me laughed at.* So I decided to date someone longer than I usually would. Women tended to cling, and I always ended up feeling claustrophobic.

I remember everything about that night, just like it was last night. I was in a club drinking in Tampa, Florida. I spotted the beautiful curvy woman as soon as she walked in. Her dark hair was swept back away from her face in curls. She sat three seats down the bar from me. I had already had three shots of whiskey. I watched as she ordered herself a shot of whiskey. She made a face as she drank it down and ordered another.

She looked at me and moved down two seats. By the time she finished her third drink, she wanted to talk. I almost left, but something about her stopped me from going. "What's your name, sweets?"

"Let's not do names green eyes."

"Okay, I'll call you gorgeous." She must want to drink her sorrows away. I must say I couldn't blame her. I was here because I had just told a woman I didn't want to get serious with anyone. I wasn't expecting all the tears and her arms clinging to me. It took another hour before I could get away from her. so I stopped to have a few drinks.

"So why are you here?" I asked.

"I'm here because I just caught my fiancé in bed with one of my employees. Why are you here?"

"Because I had trouble telling a woman I didn't want to get serious."

"Ouch, was she serious?"

"We only had three dates, but she said she loved me, and it scared the hell out of me. I thought we were enjoying each other. I didn't know she was getting serious. So I thought it would be better if I broke it off. I'm not interested in getting serious."

We talked for a couple of hours, then we got up, and both of us took a taxi to the hotel, where we made love all night. When she stepped out of her clothes, I held my breath. She was beautiful. I liked my woman curvy. She was curvy and had not an ounce of fat on her. I didn't want to make love to a woman who was all bones and worried about gaining a pound. Gorgeous was perfect. Every inch of her. As soon as I touched her, I knew this was different. My hands explored her body, and my mouth followed. She made all the right noises that set me on fire.

When I touched her lips, I pulled her naked body onto mine. My hand slipped between her thighs and touched her. My fingers parted her and slipped inside. She made a sound deep down inside that connected with me. She reached down, and her hand went around my erection. I moaned. I knew if she did that, I would come sooner than I wanted to. "Sweetheart, unless you want me coming quick, you should move your hand." She moved her hand, and I kissed my way down her body. When my tongue licked her soft spot, she pushed her body up for more. My hands cupped her ass, and I pulled her body closer, so I could give her what she wanted.

When I entered her, she was ready. I shouted out the first time I climaxed deep inside her. that was the first time of many that night. She was amazing. My body craved hers. I wanted to see if she would go out with me again. I reached over to bring her up against me, and she was gone.

Regret sat in right away. I should have gotten her name and number. All of this time, I still had her on my mind.

We had walked probably ten miles before we stopped for the night. The thing about rescuing people from prison or other dangerous areas in war-torn countries was sometimes you had to walk to where they were. Most of the places we go to have tiny airstrips, so we had to either walk or find a vehicle we could borrow from some unknown person if we were lucky enough to see a car.

"I thought you were off to Sudan," I said, shaking my pant leg. I could have sworn I felt something on my leg. I was not fond of walking in the sand; I always thought of fleas and scorpions. Hell, I didn't even know if they were in this sand.

"I will be when we finish this job. The person who has the children now has them hiding in some church, somewhere. I have to wait until the church moves them closer to civilization. I'm thinking of just going over there and getting them from the church."

"Be careful when you go over there. I've been hearing some pretty horrible stories coming from that area."

"Yeah, I've heard the same thing. I'm taking a lot of protein bars and water. Hopefully, I can get a vehicle somewhere when I get there, and we can stay out of sight if we don't have to hunt up food and water. I'm taking every gun I have plus a few knives."

"How many kids are there?"

"First, I heard there were twelve, and then I heard seven."

We set up our bedroll, and I chewed some beef jerky we always carry with us. I took a drink of water. And I went to sleep. I woke up because I heard something that shouldn't be there. It was music. Someone had to be close listening to the radio. We looked at each other. I held my finger to my lips and slipped out of my bedroll that I zipped over my head. I belly-crawled to where the noise was coming from and saw two men in a jeep, fighting with a girl crying and trying to get them off of her. I waved Conner over, and we snuck up on the vehicle. I knocked on the window, and while the two men were confused, we pulled them out of the jeep and knocked them out.

The girl started to scream, and I held my finger to my lips. She nodded. Can you speak English?"

"Yes."

"Where do you live?"

"My father kicked me out because he said he had no money for food. He sold me, so I ran away. He had money.

He knows men have been selling their daughters, and he wanted more money."

"How old are you?"

"Twelve."

"Damn, okay, we have to rescue one of our buddies. He's locked up somewhere around here. We'll take the vehicle, and you can go with us."

"If you take me to America? I'll show you where your friend is."

"We'll think about it. Let me know which way I go." Conner came back with our bedrolls and backpacks.

"You go straight." I drove for ten minutes, and the jail looked too small to be a prison. It stood right in front of us. It was dark and looked like a run-down old building. "I'll help if you take me."

"Okay, we'll take you."

"Trey, you can't take minors out of the country."

"Her father sold her to an old man."

"Okay, how are you going to help?" Conner asked her.

"My father lives here. He runs the prison. He's an evil person. I'll go inside and get your friend."

"What will happen if you get caught?"

"I will not get caught." We parked behind the building and waited for two hours before finally hearing the girl. I looked up, and there was another woman with the girl and Jackson Moore, he's a Navy Seal.

"Hey, I'm surprised you two came for me."

"We go now," the woman said, climbing into the vehicle with the girl.

"Who is she?"

"This is my mother. She's going to America with me."

"Let's go," the woman said again.

"Okay, let's go." We drove to the plane in silence. I

wondered what I would do with the mother and daughter. "Do you know anyone in America?" I asked the girl.

"Yes, my brother and sister live there. Plus my mother's sister is there also. We will be fine, so don't worry about us."

"Okay, as long as you know where you're going." I was glad we had a vehicle for the trip back to the plane. Kash waited until we loaded everyone in, then we circled the airstrip and took off. The kid and her mother slept most of the way.

I leaned back and relaxed. My eyes were shut, and gorgeous popped into my head. Why didn't I get her name? I decided right then to ask Charlie what her name was. I would have to mention her in a roundabout way, or Charlie would ask a million questions. She was always trying to help everyone. I smiled, thinking about how she questioned Ryan about Ashley. She was my cousin so I wasn't afraid to tell her to can it. Most the time she didn't pay attention anyway when I would tell her to stop questioning me.

26

MERCEDES

My face still turned red when I thought of that one crazy night of sex with a stranger. No man has ever made me feel like he did. My one night with a stranger made me feel special and all woman. I knew I would probably never see him again, but I had an ache deep down in my heart when I snuck out of the room that night. I wanted to stay, I know it sounds crazy, but that's how I felt. I have never given any man what I gave to green eyes, I felt free like I could do whatever I wanted, and that's what I did. I've never felt more like a woman than when I was with him that night. He trailed his hands over my body while he kissed me everywhere. He told me how much he loved my softness. He said my breast fit perfectly in his large hands. He turned me over and kissed me all the way down my body to my feet.

He touched my body as if it belonged to him. Like he was proud to say I was his. He told me repeatedly how beautiful I was. he said I fit him perfectly, and I did. He was tall, and his shoulders were broad. There wasn't an ounce of fat on his body. I wanted to keep him. Then I remembered I had a fiancé I needed to break up with, and green eyes didn't want a serious relationship. I was as bad as the woman he broke up with that night. I knew how she fell in love with him so fast.

That one night with a stranger made me feel more than I have ever felt. I didn't even know his name, and when I looked at him, he was beautiful. That's all my mind could think of to describe him. I could feel my face burning, and instead of doing what I wanted to do, I left. But I never forgot him. Even if I hadn't come up pregnant, I still would have remembered him, and now every time I looked at Penny and see those beautiful green eyes. I thanked him. I was so happy when I saw my daughter's eyes and they were the same green as my one-night stand.

I broke it off with the cheating bastard I was engaged to marry and realized almost too late that I didn't love him. I had green eyes to thank for that. I changed a lot of things after that night. I got rid of half my staff I didn't need. My ex-fiancé was my manager. He did the hiring, and before I called it off with him, I made sure his name was off of everything to do with Mercy Chino, the singer. I found out he was stealing a lot of my money. At the same time, he had me working my ass off. I hired a new company to handle my money. I got a new manager. I made sure he couldn't touch anything that belonged to me. Then I came home to my family and had my sweet daughter. She was the best thing in my life. I still did concerts, but not as many. I was a pop star, I had to stay on the scene, or I would be forgotten.

When I showed up at Charlie and Hunter's wedding and saw green eyes, I almost fainted dead away. I watched him from behind some bushes before I realized what I was doing, then I decided to ignore him and act like I didn't know who he was. I did find out his name was Trey Cooper.

He worked with Hunter and the Army Rangers. They rescued people. I thought that job was perfect for him. After all, he rescued me that night. I know I should have told him Penny was his daughter, but I chickened out. I didn't want him to think I expected him to change his life because of Penny. I also wanted to keep Penny to myself.

My nanny, who is also my bodyguard, opened the door to the nursery. "You don't look like you're ready."

"Ready for what?"

"Did you forget you have a concert in the park tonight?"

"That's tonight? I did forget. Penny has a fever?"

"She's fine babies get warm once in a while. That doesn't mean she's sick. Get ready. I'll take care of Penny. When we leave, your mother will watch her."

When I took Penny in for a check-up, I met Ron Hornik. He was a nurse who worked in the doctor's office. He wanted to do something else. I asked him if he wanted to be my bodyguard and part-time nanny. He agreed, and here we are a year and a half later. He went everywhere with us. He was a boxer in college. I felt like he could take care of anything that came his way.

"Mercy, let's go," Ron called out. He also made sure I was where I needed to be always.

"Here I come," I said, kissing Penny one more time before leaving. I was giving this concert with other artists to raise money for Mary's house. We want to be able to build another complex for abused women. I got involved with Mary's house when Charlie introduced me to her friends Ainsley and Lara. The park was packed. I didn't know how so many people could squeeze onto the park grounds, but they did. I had my pop singer clothes on. There wasn't much to it, but my audience loved what I wore. With my body dancing all over the stage, these clothes were easier to dance in. And it was so hot in Tampa right now I was glad I was wearing almost nothing.

The audience sang along with me on my last song. I was signing autographs, and there were so many people I couldn't breathe. Someone grabbed my wrist hard, and they squeezed it like they wouldn't let it go. I panicked and looked around for Ron. I could see him talking to a woman he was laughing with her. When I screamed his name I saw him pushing through the crowd to get to me. He called out my name as I was pulled into a crowd of men who blocked my view from seeing where Ron was. I screamed his name over and over. I heard him shouting for me. I saw him just for an instant before someone hit him over the head, and he went down. I fought with all that was in me to get away from these men. I knew I was going to be taken. My baby girl flashed before my eyes.

Someone pulled me into the dark behind the trees and threw something over my head. I couldn't scream because they put tape over my mouth and held my arms down. *I'm so sorry, Penny. I will get away from these men. I promise. God, please don't let Ron be dead. Help him, please.* I was so glad I had changed into my jeans and tee-shirt. *What was going on? Why would they take me? They must want money. I would give them money. If only they would remove this tape so I could tell them.* I was thrown into what I assumed was the trunk of a car. I started praying. *Oh no, what if Penny has to grow up without her mommy. I should have introduced her to her daddy.*

I must have blacked out for a while. I woke up and could hear men shouting. "We brought you, Mercy Chino. You can have her for twenty thousand dollars. Here she is. Give us our money. We need that money to start our business."

"What business is that? Dealing drugs. Get the hell out

of here. Don't touch her again. Leave her where she is. I'll have all of your heads on a platter."

"You're mistaken if you think I'm leaving her here with you. She goes with us." I heard a ping and knew it was a gunshot. I didn't dare let them know I was awake. I wanted to scream, but my mouth still had tape on it. I was so scared I knew I had to think; I had to get away. There was no one else, only me. Then I was picked up and thrown over someone's shoulder. I started kicking. I was determined to get away from these men. I know they killed the other guy; I heard the shot. I was thrown to the ground and kicked.

"He didn't want to pay for you, so we'll find someone else who will pay for you." I was picked up and hit until I was knocked out.

27

TREY

We had just gotten back and were at Angel's home in Tampa when Ainsley ran to Angel and threw her arms around him, crying. "What's the matter? Where is the baby?"

"The baby is fine. Mom has her. Mercy has been kidnapped, Ron is in the hospital, and someone stabbed him and then hit him over the head. Her family wants to know if you guys can talk to them."

"You guys feel up to helping find Mercy Chino?"

"That name sounds familiar," I said, looking at Ainsley

"She is a famous pop singer. Her name is Mercedes Pachino. Everyone calls her Mercy, and she shortens her last name to Chino. She has a baby girl. We have to find her," she said, crying.

"We'll talk to her family and see what's happening. Have they heard anything?"

"No, not one word. Penny wants her mommy," Ainsley cried.

"Ainsley, do you want to ride with us?"

"No, I just got home. I'll call and tell them you are on your way over there."

We only drove for about ten minutes when Angel pulled up to an electric fence and pushed the buzzer. The gate opened, and as we moved inside, eight people were standing out there waiting for us. I saw the man who stood next to gorgeous at the wedding, and my heart knew this had something to do with her.

Angel hugged everyone and then shook the hand of the man who held the baby that day. "Ron, I thought you were in the hospital. Can you tell me what happened?"

"There was a concert in the park to help raise money for Mary's House. The place was packed. Mercy was signing autographs. I told her not to leave my sight. She stood up so we could go. She wanted to get home to Penny because Mercy thought she felt warm before we left.

"I should have kept hold of her. I shouldn't have allowed her to get more than three feet away. When I realized those men were pushing her from me, I shouted her name. I heard her scream. I tried getting to her, and someone stabbed me, then they hit me with something. I felt myself falling. I knew she couldn't get away from those men. I think it was the cartel. I couldn't swear to it, but I believe it was. Just the way they looked. I'm sure I'm wrong but I just don't know."

I saw the ladies crying. The elder one looked to be in her late eighties. It looked like she would fall if she didn't sit down. "Why don't we all go inside and sit down? We will start from the top and go over everything again. I knew gorgeous was the kidnapped woman. This must then be her husband. She married the jerk who cheated on her. I already hated him before I sat down across from him. Then he got back up and walked further into the house. He came back carrying the baby.

"Tell me about your wife? Do you think she would know what to do if the cartel had her?"

"Mercy isn't my wife. I'm her bodyguard slash nanny. But most of all, I'm her friend. This is Penny, her daughter. He turned, and I looked into eyes identical to mine. I closed my eyes, and Conner, Angel, and Kash all looked at me. They saw what I saw. "Do you have a photo of Mercy?"

"She's a famous singer, you've never seen her."

Conner shook his head. "If she doesn't sing country Trey wouldn't know who she was. When Ron came back carrying her photo, I put my hand over my eyes. My baby was three feet from me. I looked at the baby. Where is Penny's daddy?"

"I've never asked," Ron said as he looked closely at me. I got up and walked outside. She saw me at the wedding she must have. She could have told me I had a child. I thought back to that night and our conversation. She knew I didn't want a serious relationship. That's why she said nothing. I heard someone behind me and turned. The elderly lady stood there.

"So you're Penny's daddy."

"Yeah, I think I am. I'll find her mommy," I walked back inside. "Let's go talk to the cartel." I noticed Ron stand, and I shook my head. "You guard Penny; we'll find Mercy." The name fit her perfectly. I was crying for Mercy before the night with her was over, and I was ready to go again, but I woke up alone. I walked over to where Penny patted Ron on the back and held out my hands. She almost jumped into my arms. I held her close to me, and I knew I would give my life to protect this baby. She was beautiful, and she had my eyes. She looked at me then she kissed me right on the mouth. I blinked so I wouldn't show how shook up I was.

"Penny, my sweet baby girl, I'm your daddy."

"Dada."

"Yes, dada." I kissed my baby and then handed her back to Ron. I turned and walked out of the room. The men stared at me. "Are you going to stand there, or are we leaving?"

We were headed to Marcus Marcelli's place in Angel's truck when Conner turned to me. "You had frigging sex with Mercy Chino all night, and you didn't know who she was. God, you had the best sex in your life with the beautiful Mercy. She can move that beautiful body of hers all over that stage and have every man in the room wanting her, and you didn't know her. I've been to three of her concerts."

"Shut the fuck up. She is the mother of my baby girl. I want you to forget everything I told you about that night. I was drunk when I told you, so keep it from your mind."

"How the hell am I supposed to do that? You told me how soft her skin was. You told me how she tasted."

"Conner, I'm serious. Get it out of your brain." We pulled up to the gate that kept Marcelli from the world. When we buzzed the gate, men came out from the trees. Their guns were trained on us. "What's happened," I asked. I saw one of the men we've dealt with before and addressed him.

"Marcus Marcelli was shot. It was the cartel from down south. He said they had Mercy Chino, and he tried to stop them from taking her.

"Where is he? I want to talk to him," I demanded.

"He's not taking visitors. He could have died. They left him for dead when they left. We'll take care of them. You don't have to get involved."

"That woman is the mother to my baby girl, don't tell me I don't need to do anything. I want to talk to Marcus."

"Follow me. Let me tell him Mercy is your baby's

mother. Then you can talk to him. Don't get him riled up, or he'll split open his stitches again."

We don't usually hang out with the cartel, but things changed when Marcus took over from his uncle two years ago. He tried keeping things low so as not to cause trouble with the people who lived here. He didn't do any human trafficking, or drug dealing. I don't actually know what he does besides the horse tracks. I've seen his horses. I heard shouting when we walked into his home. I looked around and was surprised to see how comfortable it looked.

"Tell them to get in here. Fuck hurry, I'm going with them."

We walked into the room, and Marcus was dressed and laid on top of the bed. Marcus, stay where you are," Angel said as he walked to the bed. "Where did the bullet hit you?"

"In the chest, it laid me out cold. That bastard had a silencer on his gun. I'm going to kill all of those fuckers. He wanted me to buy Mercy for twenty thousand. I would have if I knew what his plans were. I thought if I told him to get away from her, he would leave. I fucking didn't think he would shoot me. Now, what the hell is this all about Mercy being the mama to your baby?" He asked, looking at Trey.

"It means I'm going to kill that bastard. Where are they?"

"I have some men on it. I think it's better if the Rangers don't get involved."

"We are already involved. Where did those men take her?"

"I'm almost positive she's in Mexico. Probably the jungle. They would know they'll be hunted down. All of those men know they are dead men. I hope someone else has the woman by now. My plane is waiting for us. He went to raise himself, and Angel stopped him.

"Let me see your wound."

"Why?"

"Because I want to see if you will be able to make the trip. What if we have to go through the jungle? Are you going to be able to handle hiking?"

"We won't have to hike. I have a home and plenty of vehicles in Mexico."

"Let's go," I said, turning around and walking out of the room. I was finished with talking. We needed to hurry if Mercy had a chance of being rescued. I stopped and looked at Kash. "Will you take the family to Maine? I don't want to leave Penny without a guard."

"They have a home in Maine. I'll have all of them waiting there for when you rescue Mercy. Trey, don't forget you are a prince. You can call in a lot of favors. Now would be a good time to do it."

"I know. I'll call Charlie. She's so much better at that than I am. I'll call her right now," I dialed my phone. "Charlie, it's me, Trey."

"Hey, are you on your way home?"

"Not yet, I have something to tell you. The cartel took Mercedes Pachino. Marcus believes she's in Mexico. I was hoping you could call in some favors and have people looking for her before we get there."

"What! Did you say my friend was kidnapped?"

"Yes, and her daughter Penny is my daughter."

"Wait, did you say Mercy's been kidnapped? What do you mean Penny is your daughter?"

"I'll explain everything when I see you. Call people and have them start looking for her."

"I'll do it right now. Trey, I have to tell you I don't have many contacts in Mexico. You have to find her."

"Charlie, Kash will bring the rest of the family to Maine.

Can you please keep an eye on my daughter? I'm going to call my mom and have her come stay with us."

"Of course, I will. Trey, you have to find her before it's too late."

I hung up the phone, and Marcus watched me. "Are you related to Hunter's wife?"

"Yeah, we are cousins."

"So, what side of her family are you from?"

"Why?"

"Because I want to know if you're a prince."

"It doesn't matter if I am or not. I'm a Ranger. That's all those men have to worry about."

DEAR READER.

Thank you, for your continued support. I really appreciate that you read my books.

If you can please leave me a review for this book, I would appreciate it enormously.

Your reviews allow me to get validation I need to keep going as an Indie author.

Just a moment of your time is all that is needed. I will try my best to give you the

best books I can write.

Join me on social media Follow me on BookBub
https://www.bookbub.com/profile/susie-mciver

NEWSLETTER   SIGN   UP   HTTP://BIT.LY/
SUSIEMCIVER_NEWSLETTER

FACEBOOK PAGE: www.facebook.com/SusieMcIverAuthor/

. . .

FACEBOOK GROUP: www.facebook.com/
groups/SusieMcIverAuthor/

HTTPS://WWW.SUSIEMCIVER.COM/

ARMY RANGERS SPECIAL OPS
  KASH
  My Book
  ANGEL
  My Book
  MATT
  My Book
  JAX
  My Book
  RYAN
  My Book
  TREY
  My Book
  CONNER
  My Book
  ASHER
  My Book

BAND OF NAVY SEALS
  KILLIAN BOOK 1
  My Book

. . .

ROWAN BOOK 2
My Book

ZANE BOOK 3
My Book

STORM BOOK 4
https://www.amazon.com/dp/B08Y7C9D4Z

ASH BOOK 5
My Book

JONAH BOOK 6
My Book

KANE BOOK 7
My Book

AUSTIN BOOK 8
My Book
LUKE
My Book
RYES
My Book

Printed in Great Britain
by Amazon